CAPTURED
MOMENTS

Frances E. Pitts

Green Ivy Publishing
1 Lincoln Centre
18W140 Butterfield Road
Suite 1500
Oakbrook Terrace IL 60181-4843
www.greenivybooks.com

Captured Moments/Frances E. Pitts

ISBN: 978-1-946043-63-4
Ebook: 978-1-946043-64-1

Chapter 1

The Early Years

Jodi Bennett had just turned eighteen. The summer was in full swing, and she couldn't wait to spend time on her greatest love: her artwork.

Ever since she was a little girl, she had loved to play with paints and paper. She loved the way some of the colors would change and run together. She had her pictures all over the walls of her room. Now, as she had gotten older, she had progressed to using oils and acrylics. People who had seen her work told her that she was unusually talented.

Jodi's dream was to go to art school and learn all the techniques she so envied. This fall, her dream would come true. She would go to The School of the Arts in Atlanta. It had been difficult saving her money for the tuition so that she could attend. Her parents had told her to save as much as she could, and they would pay the rest. Atlanta was close enough that she would probably be able to come home often.

The Bennett family consisted of Jodi, her parents Susan and Alex, and her ten-year-old little brother Jesse. Last but not least was Jesse's little, white terrier Sparky, who stuck like glue to Jesse wherever he went. They lived in a small, coastal town in Georgia called Windy Point. It was a laid-back community of people who never seemed to be in a hurry. They took time to enjoy life as it came. The town wasn't large, but what it lacked in size, it made up for in its scenic locations. People loved the fact that it wasn't an upscale town. It was just big enough for you to find what you needed when you needed it. Tourists who happened to find it always made a point to come back. There was just such a "homey" feel to it. The people who lived there always made you feel as though you were some long-lost relative who had finally made your way back home. The Bennett family owned and operated a bed and breakfast called the Sea Bird, which people told them felt like home. For that reason, the Bennetts advertised the Sea Bird as having "left a candle in the window for you."

The inn had belonged to Alex's parents until their passing. His family had always known that they wanted to continue on with the inn, just as the grandparents had done. The wonderful meals that the guests enjoyed were prepared by their longtime cook, Sarah Ashby. Sarah was family, even if she wasn't related to them. She was a portly woman who always wore an apron and a big smile. She loved to cook, and everyone bragged about the amazing things that came out of her kitchen.

The large, two-storied, shingled house was skirted on all four sides with porches and presented a beautiful, peaceful view of the ocean. There were ten bedrooms in this big, old home, three of which were occupied by the Bennetts. The others were rented throughout most of the warmer months. The home was surrounded by trees and lovely flower beds that Alex always managed to keep looking in tip-top condition. Guests enjoyed sitting in the many rocking chairs along the front porch where they could enjoy the balmy sea breezes, morning coffee, and perhaps a sweet tea or two. The house was set behind a long row of sand dunes with the ocean just a short stroll away, and it was a pleasant walk into Windy Point. Renters enjoyed the close proximity to whatever they might wish to see or do.

Jodi's bedroom was at the rear of the house. There was a dormer window where she set up her easel and painting supplies. The light was good there, and she knew she would not be in the way when she was painting. People had told Jodi that she should never have a problem selling her work. She could visualize so many scenes that it was always hard to choose what to paint next. The scenes began to take shape in her mind even before the painting began.

It was early June, and the day was warm with only a light breeze blowing. Jodi sat on a bench in the town park. The park was small but a great place to sit and relax.

When a ball struck her foot, she gently kicked it away without even thinking. The ball rolled over towards the children who had been playing with it. They squealed and kept on playing. She loved watching them play. They gave her ideas for more paintings. She paid special attention to their movements and the expressions on their faces. Painting was always on Jodi's mind. Even when she was asleep, she dreamed of scenes on her canvas.

She thought about the most recent painting she had started. Jodie had begun working on it soon after graduation. It was a beach scene depicting two small children playing in the shallow water as the waves lapped the shore. The painting had taken days to do, and she hoped that it would be finished soon. Children were so easy to paint. They weren't like adults, who always seemed to care how they looked or what people would think of them. They looked at things with innocent awe. It didn't matter if their hair blew out of place or if their faces were dirty. They enjoyed life.

She watched as a little girl hung upside down from the monkey bars. The secret was to somehow capture them on canvas when they weren't aware you were watching. This painting just needed some little, extra touches to bring it to life. She pictured the canvas in her mind and studied its content.

I should take some photographs of these kids so I can capture some of their movements and expressions, she thought.

She mentally made a note to bring her camera the next time she went for a walk. Jodi was like that, always writing notes to herself and making lists of things she wanted to accomplish. She sometimes drove her family nutty with her habit of organizing everything she did. Her bedroom had tacky notes everywhere.

Somehow, she kept up with them all. Her motto was, "Think it, see it, organize it, paint it."

The Bennett children had always lived at the Sea Bird. Having people in their home was commonplace for them. They had grown up hardly knowing a stranger. "Always someone new to meet," they said.

Chapter 2

"Mom! I'm home!" said Jodie.

Susan Bennett was in the large dining room, getting ready to set the table for the dinner guests. Everyone loved this room. It had huge windows that let the sun filter inside. Sarah was in the big kitchen, doing the last-minute touch-ups to the meal.

"I'll be there in just a second to help you," Jodi said as she put her things away.

She knew she had to help her mother with the meals. It was the time of year when the number of guests was at its peak. She didn't mind, though, because having new people to talk to was always exciting for her. It was almost like having family come to visit.

As Jodi placed the silverware on the table, Jesse came in.

"What movie's playing in Windy Point?" asked Jesse.

"I believe it's another western," Jodi said.

"Oh, wow! Mom, may I go?"

"You can go if your sister goes with you," said Susan.

"Aw, nuts, Mom," said Jesse. "I'm not a baby!"

"I know you aren't, Jesse, but I'd feel better if you didn't go alone."

"Then both of us can go," said Jodi. "Okay, Mom?"

Jodi always took up for her younger brother. He had friends when school was in session, but during the summertime, there weren't many boys his age around. Jodi didn't like to see him left out of things. She had waited a long time to have a sibling, and he really was a good little brother.

"Okay," said Susan. "As long as you go to the earliest show. Did you know we will have new guests at supper? Jack and Meredith Parker are joining us tonight. They have a son about your age, Jesse. They will be arriving shortly."

Jesse thought this was great. It wasn't too often anyone came that might be good company for him.

Jodi turned her head toward the window. Was that a car door closing out front?

Alex walked into the front foyer carrying suitcases as the Parkers arrived.

"How was your trip?" he asked as Jack Parker signed his family in.

"It was great!" said Jack. "We made good time driving down from New York."

"Wow! New York?" said Jesse.

Meredith Parker stood waiting at the desk with their young son. "Yes son," she said. "It's a long, long drive down to Georgia. This is our son, Sammy. What is your name?"

"My name is Jesse, and I'm ten," said Jesse. "And this is my dog Sparky. How old are you, Sammy?"

"I'm nine and a half," said Sammy.

The little dog wagged his tail so hard he couldn't be still. Sparky was always ready for more attention. He jumped up onto Sammy's legs and licked his hands.

"Down, boy!" said Jesse.

"It's okay," said Sammy. "I wish I had a dog like this. I don't have a dog because we live in the city and don't have a yard for one. This one is really cool."

The parents all agreed that the boys should have a great time together since they were so close in age, and it wasn't a surprise that the boys managed to sit beside each other when they ate that night. The chatter began as soon as they sat down.

The other dinner guests began gathering around the dinner table. The room was large and comfortable. It was like dining at Grandma's house. Jodi helped her mother and Sarah serve the meal while the two boys had a great time getting acquainted with each other. They discovered they both collected model airplanes.

It was going to be a fun summer for Jesse now that he had a buddy to keep him company.

"Jodi, pass those potatoes to Mr. Kensington," said Mom.

"Everything is so tasty," Mr. Kensington replied. "I don't get to eat like this too often."

During the meal, as everyone talked with each other, Jodi learned a little about the guests. John and Evelyn Barkley were from Iowa and had never seen the ocean. They were totally amazed by it. John managed a textile mill. Their little daughter, Millie, who was only four, would be sure to love the ocean, too. Emily Jenkins, who was a clothing buyer from Atlanta, was looking forward to a lazy vacation in the sun, away from her office. Robert Kensington was an author from North Carolina who wanted to scout the area for material for his new book.

One thing that really interested Jodi was the fact that Mr. Parker ran an art gallery. She wondered what he would think of her paintings. Should she dare to ask him to look at them? She decided to wait until the time was right to approach him about it.

He'll probably think I'm just an amateur, she thought, but it would be good to get an opinion from an outsider.

After dinner was over, the guests went about with their plans. The Barkleys went for a walk on the beach with Millie. Meredith and Jack Parker went out to have a mint julep on the front porch. Mr. Kensington went up to his room to plan his book. Miss Jenkins said, "I think I will read a little here in the living room. This room is so beautiful with its big fireplace."

The two Bennett children were about to leave to go to the movie in town when Susan mentioned that maybe Sammy would like to go with them.

"Jodi will watch out for him, Mrs. Parker," assured Susan, "if he would like to go. The movie is only about two blocks from here."

"I think that would be fine," said Mrs. Parker. "You stay with Jodi now, Sammy. Don't wander off."

"I will," Sammy told his mother.

Jodi, Jesse, and Sammy all headed off to Windy Point.

"Looks like the summer is off to a good start for them," said Alex.

Susan agreed, pleased to see the children happy. She had to call Sparky back to keep him from going to the movies, too.

Chapter 3

It was Saturday, and Jodi was gathering her supplies to do some painting at the beach. It had been quite a while since she had gotten time off from her chores at the Sea Bird to do this. She had gotten up early to help make cakes for the guests' desserts. She was always there when her mom needed her help. Now, she had some time for herself and, of course, time to paint.

She was excited about finishing her painting. Yesterday, it had rained and was overcast, but today was just right for painting. The day was glorious. The sun was just right. Hopefully, she would get this one finished in time for Mr. Parker to see before they went back to New York. She felt she had given it her very best effort.

The colors of the water were just right this time. She had blended in the blues and deep greens to show depth in the water. She took special care to show the movement. The sunlight reflected in the eyes of the children. All she had to do was finish up their faces, and it would be done. If she could just make this picture speak!

The smile on the little girl's face began to come alive. She had managed to catch that little sign of laughter in her eyes. She wanted to show the amazement the little boy felt as the water rushed between his toes. Now, it was there, what she wanted the viewer to see. She wanted them to see the thrill the children felt from the feel of the sun, the water, and the wet sand beneath their feet. It was all there. The children had come alive on the canvas.

Jodi was so pleased. This was what the whole painting was about—the reality of what the children felt. She could check this off of her list. She felt she had completed her best work. Jodi wondered what her next subject would be. She thought about making another list. This would be a list of subjects she wanted to paint.

Jodi had started carrying her camera with her everywhere. She took candid shots of things she had never thought about painting. The box in her room was filling with snapshots. Ideas started coming to her about what her next painting might be. Children were always her favorite subjects. Jesse and Sammy were in her lens more than ever. The two boys had become very best friends since that first night at the movies. After that, all she heard was talk about airplanes, boats, and the ocean. Of course, Sparky was there to listen to it all.

Alex was outside pulling weeds from the flower bed in the front yard when Jodi headed out onto the front steps.

"Are you headed to town?" he asked.

"Yes, Dad," she said. "Do you need me to pick up anything for you?"

"I sure could use some small nails to repair some of those shingles. Would you mind stopping by Mobley's Hardware?"

"No problem. Mom has me running a few errands for her, too. I also need to get some more paints and a new brush or two."

"Have Mom give you the money, then," he said.

About that time, Jesse and Sammy came running up from the beach. They had been out collecting seashells along the jetty.

"Look at all the shells we found this time, Jodi," said Jesse.

"Those are awesome boys," she said. "I'm heading for town. Do you guys want to tag along?"

"Sure!" said Jesse. "Hold on and let us tell our moms."

"I'll be right here waiting for you," she said.

When Jodi returned with the money, the boys were sitting on the steps waiting for her.

"Okay, Dad, we're off," said Jodi.

There was Sparky bringing up the rear. He was weaving in and out of them as they walked, excited to go along.

By the time they arrived at Mobley's Hardware, the boys had nearly talked Jodi's ears off. Sparky sat down in front of the store and waited for their return.

"You guys can look around while I get Dad's nails, okay?" said Jodi.

She walked to the counter where the nails were and saw Mr. Mobley arranging a new display.

"Hi, Jodi," said Ralph Mobley. "How are your folks doing?"

"Oh, hey, Mr. Mobley. They are just fine. We have almost a full house this week."

"That's great news. What can I help you with?"

"Dad needs some nails to repair our shingles. What size should they be?"

Ralph looked over the counter and handed her a box of nails. "These should do fine. Is there anything else you need?"

"Yes. I need to look at your paints and artist's brushes. Do you have any new ones in?"

She followed him as he went to their small area of art supplies.

"I think Mrs. Mobley told me that some came in on Thursday," he said. "Did you have anything in particular in mind?"

"I'm looking for a new sable brush. I also need some burnt sienna, cobalt blue, and some olive green."

Mr. Mobley picked out the items she needed, which she figured would do for now. Then she set about looking for the boys. She was not surprised to find them in the area where Mr. Mobley had model airplanes, boats, and cars for sale.

"Have you found something you like?" she asked. Both boys were holding boxes of the same model. The label read *Japanese Kamikaze Airplane*.

"We want these," said Jesse. "Is it one you are old enough to put together?" asked Jodi.

"Yes, it says ten years old and up," said Jesse. "If he has any trouble, I can help him."

"Okay, if you are sure."

"We 're sure, we're sure," they both said in unison.

Jodi got out her camera and snapped a picture of the two happy little boys. After picking up a few things for Mom at Sack & Go, the local grocery, the three of them marched home. Sparky ran along behind them wagging his tail, glad to be back in the group.

When they arrived home, the boys quickly raced up to Jesse's bedroom to start on their new airplanes. Sparky ran up after them to oversee the project. As an afterthought, Jesse leaned over the staircase railing and called out, "Thank you, Jodi!"

"You are both welcome," she called back.

They were great kids, and it made her feel good to see them so happy.

Chapter 4

Jodi was out on the front porch with her easel when Mr. Parker walked out with a morning cup of coffee.

"What's that you are doing?" he asked.

"I'm working on a seascape. I want to catch it in the early sunlight."

"I didn't know you were an artist," he said. "And a very good one at that."

"Well, I know I have a long way to go to be a professional, but I'm going to attend The School of the Arts in Atlanta this fall."

"That's great, but I can see you have a natural gift already."

Jodi wondered if this might be the time to ask him about her other paintings.

"I wonder," she said. "Could you or would you mind giving me your opinion on some of my other work?"

"Sure," he said. "I'd be glad to look them over. I'm not busy this morning. How about right after breakfast?"

"Awesome! As soon as I help Mom clear the dishes, we can go look at them."

Jodi couldn't wait for breakfast to be over. As soon as the last guest left the table, she was already stacking up the dishes on a tray.

"Mom, I am going to show Mr. Parker my paintings," she said. "I want his opinion on my work."

"That's great, Jodi. You go ahead. Sarah and I can finish up here."

"You are the best, Mom," said Jodi.

She almost ran back into the living room to find Mr. Parker. "We can go up now if you are ready," she said.

As soon as Mr. Parker entered her room he could see talent. Everywhere he looked, he saw paintings of beaches, parks, shorelines, and sunsets, and, of course, most of them had children in them.

"Well, I can tell you one thing," he said. "You could have buyers right now wanting this kind of work."

"Really?" She almost blushed. "I loved painting them, but I didn't think they were that special."

"You underestimate yourself, Jodi. I heard in town that they are having an art gallery showing for the Fourth of July Celebration next month. You should apply."

"Do you really think I am that good? There will be lots of professional artists showing there."

"I say go for it!" he said. "What have you got to lose? This is a great way to get your foot in the door. Get your name out there, Jodi!"

"You are making me be excited about it, Mr. Parker! I think I will do it!"

"That's the spirit!" he said. "Pick out your very best ones and possibly do a few more. Think about how you want to display them. Sometimes, that's the key. I'll be glad to help you while we are here."

"Thanks so much, Mr. Parker. This means so much to me."

◊◊◊

After spending the morning talking with Mr. Parker, Jodi was so excited she had to go tell her best friend Mandy at the sandwich shop in town.

"Mom, I am going to see Mandy," she said. "I won't be too long."

"Okay, just be sure to be home in time to help with lunch," said Mom.

"I will," she called back as she hopped onto her bicycle and rode off towards Windy Point.

Mandy was sitting at a corner booth folding napkins when Jodi arrived. Her parents, Phil and Dianne Adams, ran the sandwich shop called the Sand Dollar. Jodi helped out part-time when there weren't many guests at the inn.

"Mandy, I am *so* excited!" said Jodi. "One of our guests, Mr. Parker, who runs an art gallery in New York, says that I should apply to enter the art showing for the Fourth of July event in town. He saw my paintings and thinks they are good enough to sell!"

"Jodi!" Mandy said. "I've been telling you that all along. You know you do a great job. Everyone says so. Now, what can I do to help you?"

"Well, the first thing, I guess, is to get an application for the showing. Where do I get that?"

"I think Mrs. Mobley is in charge of that," said Mandy. "Try asking at their store."

Jodi reached over and took a pile of napkins and started folding. "I will need something to display the paintings on. Maybe Dad can build that for me. Frames. I need frames for the paintings."

"I saw some frames at the thrift store last week. I'm sure you could find enough to do most of them. They might just need a little touch-up work. I could do that for you."

"Thanks so much, Mandy. I will have a lot to do between now and the show. I am so lucky to have a good friend like you."

Mandy smirked at her as Jodi snapped her picture.

After Jodi and Mandy had their discussion, Jodi headed over to Mobley's Hardware.

"Child, I was wondering why you haven't come in to ask about this sooner," said Martha Mobley. "Everyone who has seen your work loves it. You should do very well at the showing."

"Thanks, Miss Martha," said Jodi, "but I am a little nervous about it. It's a lot to get done before the Fourth."

"Sure it is, but you will make it. I've heard about you and all your lists." She chuckled.

Jodi got the application sheet from her and headed for home. "Thanks, Miss Martha!" she called back.

"Good luck to you, Jodi!" she said.

Chapter 5

Three days later, a letter arrived from the Fourth of July Planning Committee saying that she would be a part of the gallery showing. She knew that there would be no time to spare. Jodi had asked her dad about building a frame of some sort to hold her paintings.

"Sure, I'll see what I can come up with," he said. "It shouldn't take long."

Mom suggested that they cover it with lattice work and paint it white. This would make a pretty backdrop for her work. Mr. Parker said he would help her to price her paintings. This was a difficult decision for Jodi. He assured her that people really would be willing to pay her for her talent. She had never looked at it that way. Jodi only thought of painting as something she loved doing.

Mandy had managed to find over twenty-five frames. They got together on Monday afternoon and began sanding and painting any that needed work. They were almost finished, and Mandy promised she would do the few that were left.

Every chance she got, Jodi worked on her paintings. She spent many hours at the beach working on sunsets or children building sand castles. She watched dogs playing on the beach chasing their owners. Sometimes the dog was Sparky, and the kids were Jesse and Sammy. Of course, she managed to get a picture of them. She took in every scene she could imagine.

Walking out the back door, Jodi found Dad hammering away on a large frame in the backyard.

"What do you think of it?" he asked.

"Looks fine to me. Will it stand up by itself or do we have to anchor it?" Jodi asked.

"I will have the whole thing mounted on my flat trailer. All we have to do is park it. You will need some steps for it, and that should be it. I'll get those made too. I will be there to help you get it set up, so don't worry about that. It will also have a tarp roof attached to it, so you won't be in the direct sun."

"It sounds like you have thought of everything. This is going to be awesome, Dad! I bought the lattice work yesterday, and I can get that painted this afternoon. Mandy and I are finishing up all the frames, and then we can put the art in them after they all dry."

"Sounds like everyone is on the ball," said Dad.

"I know. I can't wait!"

Later that afternoon, Jodi was working hard at painting the lattice work.

"I think it needs some kind of sign telling who the artist is," said Mom. "Let me be in charge of that, okay?"

"Sure Mom, I would appreciate that."

"Don't worry," Dad said. "When we get through with this, it will be shooting off sky rockets and sparklers!"

"Oh Dad, not *that* flashy, please!" said Jodi.

Susan spent the rest of the day gathering fabrics to make her banner.

"I think it should have some starfish and seabirds on it," she said. "What do you think?"

"Anything you do will be just fine, Mom," said Jodi. "I like your taste."

"So skyrockets and sparklers it is then, right?" she said with a grin.

"Mom!"

"I'm just kidding, Jodi," said Mom.

Chapter 6

Jesse and Sammy were out on the beach watching the waves rise and fall and crash onto the shore.

"Wow, look at that one!" said Sammy. "I wonder if a boat could go over one like that."

Sparky, who followed them whenever they let him, barked at the big wave.

"I don't know," said Jesse. "I've never taken a boat out. My Dad has a small rowboat. He keeps it up under the house out back, but I'm not allowed to use it."

"Really? Why not?" said Sammy. "I bet we could row one."

"Dad told me it wasn't safe for little kids. We need to have an adult with us."

"I think it would be lots of fun, though," said Sammy.

"Yeah, maybe, but I would get in trouble if I tried it," said Jesse.

Sparky kept chasing the water back every time the waves came in. They walked down the beach, throwing broken shells into the ocean as they went. Sammy was tracing lines in the sand with a stick as he followed behind Jesse.

"Can you show me where the boat is when we get back?" said Sammy.

"Yeah, I'll show you, but we can't use it," said Jesse. "I'm hungry."

"Me too," said Sammy.

Together, they ran over the sand dunes back to the house with Sparky barking at their heels.

◊◊◊

"Make sure you get all that sand off of you before you two come inside!" called Sarah as the boys came in for lunch. "And make sure Sparky stays outside. It looks like he's been rolling in the wet sand again."

She was making some chicken salad for sandwiches, a luscious chocolate cake for dessert, and a fresh pitcher of sweet tea for lunch.

"Lunch will be ready shortly," Sarah told them.

"We will be ready for it," said the boys.

The Barkleys, Miss Jenkins, and the Parkers were all there gathering for lunch. Mr. Kensington would be having lunch in town. They were all talking about the upcoming celebration for the Fourth. Mr. Bennett told his family he had heard that Sam, down at the docks, was talking with Mr. Kensington. He had been talking with lots of the locals for some ideas for his book. Everyone was wondering what his topic would finally be.

As they sat around the table, Jodi told Miss Jenkins that she would be going to school in Atlanta this fall.

"Oh really?" said Miss Jenkins. "I don't know if you would be interested, but I own a small, two-bedroom apartment fairly close to that school that I would be more than glad to rent to you while you are there. It's big enough to have a roommate if you need one. Here is my agent's name and number if you think you might like to look at it." She handed Jodi her card.

"I'll talk with Mom and Dad about it," said Jodi. "Thank you."

"Atlanta is a wonderful city," she said. "But you will also be glad to come back to this peaceful place. I think I will plan next year's vacation here, too."

"We would be more than happy to have you back here with us," said Susan.

"Be sure to light the candle for me," laughed Miss Jenkins.

"Oh, we will, we will," laughed the Bennetts.

The Barkleys came in leading little Millie by the hand. She was carrying a new sand pail and shovel.

"I'll just bet you have been digging up the beach, haven't you?" said Susan.

"I almost dug down to the bottom of the world!" Millie said.

"Well I hope you left some dirt down there for China!" said Alex.

"We were really having the best time out there," said Mr. Barkley.

"The water is beautiful, and the sunsets are just glorious," said Mrs. Barkley. "We will have so much to tell our friends when we get back to Iowa. I'm sure Frank and Joanne Peterson would love to come with us next year."

"The more the merrier," said Susan.

"We'll be right back down for lunch as soon as we change out of our swimsuits," Evelyn said.

"Sarah, that chocolate cake was awesome," said Jack Parker. "If I weren't watching my waistline, I would have another slice."

"Go right ahead," said Sarah. "You can just walk another mile down the beach." She chuckled her way back into the kitchen.

◊◊◊

Sammy and Jesse went outside to the backyard.

"Show me the little boat, Jesse," said Sammy.

"There it is," said Jesse, pointing under the porch. "Dad hasn't used it in a long time."

21

Under the edge of the back porch, the little rowboat lay upside down with the oars on top of the boat.

"That's so cool!" said Sammy.

"I'd rather ride the waves on my boogie board," said Jesse.

Sparky ran up to Jesse with a ball in his mouth.

"Looks like you want to play catch, huh Sparky?"

After they tossed the ball around and had Sparky bring it back a few times, they decided to go up to Jesse's room and play with their model airplanes.

"We need to find another one to work on, don't we?" said Jesse.

"Yeah, maybe we can talk Dad into taking us into Windy Point," Sammy said.

"Do you think he would? My dad is busy nailing shingles."

"Sure. Let's go ask."

The boys found Mr. Parker sitting in one of the front porch rockers reading the newspaper.

"Dad!" said Sammy. "Will you take us into Windy Point? Jesse and I want to find another model to work on."

He thought for a moment and then said, "Well I don't think your mother has anything planned this afternoon, so I don't see why not."

"Okay," said Jesse. "I have to go and let Mom know I'm going."

As usual, Sparky found them before they left and off he ran behind them. Mr. Parker had to keep up the pace because the boys would run a while, then walk a while. Sparky decided it was easier to follow Mr. Parker than the boys.

"Are they tiring you out Sparky?" he asked. "I think I know the feeling." He chuckled to himself.

When they arrived at Mobley's Hardware, the boys ran straight to the model section of the store.

"Well, I guess they know what they want," said Mr. Mobley.

"Yeah, they both have a special interest in model airplanes," said Mr. Parker.

"I remember," said Mr. Mobley.

This time, Jesse and Sammy picked different models. Jesse found an old World War I biplane, and Sammy found a model of Howard Hughes's Spruce Goose.

"You two sure got some interesting choices this time," commented Mr. Parker.

"Yeah, Dad, aren't they cool?" said Sammy. "Can you help us if we have trouble putting them together?"

"I think that might be arranged," said his dad.

After they had paid for the planes, they left the store. At first, they didn't see Sparky anywhere. They were sure he had followed them right to the door.

"I think I see what happened to him," said Mr. Parker, pointing.

There underneath the bench was Sparky, sound asleep.

"You guys wore him out on the way into town. He needed a nap."

"Come on, Sparky," said Jesse. "Let's go home, boy."

Up Sparky jumped and licked Jesse in the face. All the way home, the boys talked about their new models and how much fun it was going to be putting them together.

Chapter 7

It was Wednesday, and Jodi only had until Friday to finish up her display for the art gallery. Saturday was July Fourth.

Jodi had just finished helping Mom clear the luncheon dishes when Mandy came in to help her put her paintings into the frames.

"Hey there, Mandy," said Mrs. Bennett. "I haven't seen too much of you this summer. Has the Sand Dollar been busy?"

"Hi, Mrs. Bennett," said Mandy. "It sure has. Mama says she may have to hire some more help."

"Well, I guess that's a good thing then, isn't it?"

"Yes, it's good we have a lot of business, but Mama never gets to take a break."

"That's the nature of the beast isn't it?" sighed Mrs. Bennett. "I do know that both you and Jodi are a very big help. I know when Jodi goes to school this fall I will surely miss her."

"I know you will, Mom," said Jodi. "I'll miss you and Dad, too. Of course, I'll miss that little brother of mine, too. It won't be forever, though, Mom. You know I will be home fairly often."

"I'm going to miss her too," said Mandy a little sadly.

"I'll keep in touch, Mandy. I promise I will."

The girls went up to Jodi's room and began putting the artwork into the frames.

"Wow, don't they look awesome!" said Mandy.

"The frames do make a difference don't they?" said Jodi.

"Jodi, you haven't signed your work! Why not?"

"I never thought about it. I guess I should if I'm going to try to sell them."

"Of course, you should!"

After the work was done, they counted thirty-two paintings total.

"I think you have a painting of about any subject anyone could want," said Mandy. "I especially love this one with the girl and boy playing at the water's edge."

"It's funny you should say that, because that is my favorite too," Jodi said.

"Their eyes really tell the story," said Mandy as she leaned over to look at it more closely.

"Thank you, Mandy. That's exactly what I was trying to do."

Mr. Parker had chosen these as her best works. She hoped he was right. Jodi began adding her signature to the paintings as Mandy had suggested. It was all becoming very real to her now. It was her very first showing.

Dad had already mounted the display frame with the lattice work onto his trailer and had done a great job. He was almost finished making the steps up to the trailer. The tarp just had to be connected to the frame after they parked the trailer. Jodi had painted the lattice bright white. It was sure to show off her work. Mom was just finishing up the sewing on the beautiful banner for the front. It read, *Jodi Bennett—Windy Point's Own Artist,* and it had appliqués of little starfish and seashells all over it. Susan was clearly proud of her daughter and hoped that this would be a real beginning for her.

"I think it's turning out really nice," Jack Parker told Jodi.

"I can't believe this is all happening, Mr. Parker!" said Jodi. "If it weren't for you, I never would have had the nerve to even try this."

"Jodi, it really would have been a great loss if you hadn't. You have such a gift, even without formal training. I was amazed when I first saw your work. This is just the first step. You'll see. I expect to see your work someday in a gallery in New York. Mark my words. Just let a few outsiders see what you can do. Your teachers at the Institute will tell you."

"Thank you," said Jodi. "I can't tell you what all this means to me. It has been a lifelong dream of mine."

Jodi thought about the few things she still had left to do on her list. There was one more painting that she was hoping to have completed in time for the showing. It was of Sammy out on the beach. He was looking out over the waves at a small boat that was passing by, using his hand to keep the sun from shining in his eyes. His blond hair was blowing across his forehead. In his hand, Sammy held a starfish he had found on the beach. The smile on his face said it all. He loved the ocean. He loved the sun and the sand. Most of all, he loved the thought of being on the ocean.

"I still can't quite get it right," said Jodi, looking at the incomplete painting. "Something is missing. I may have to put this one aside for another time."

The rest of her day was spent making sure she had cash on hand for making change, checking her pricing, and making sure all the paintings had hooks to hang from. Did she have enough bags for her customers? All the while, she was checking off things from yet another list.

Mrs. Bennett came in to show her how the new banner had turned out.

"Oh, Mom! It's terrific!" she said. "Your banner is art, too!"

"Thank you, sweetheart," Mom said. "I had fun making it for you. I just have to have something to hang it by. I'll check with Dad about that."

Chapter 8

The Celebration

Saturday was finally here. It was The Fourth of July.

"I thought it would never get here," Jodi told her mom. They had gotten up early so they would have plenty of time to get everything ready for the gallery.

"I know you are excited, but please, just sit down and eat some breakfast," said Mom. "It's going to be a long day for you."

"Okay, Mom. I'm just going over some of my lists to make sure I haven't forgotten anything."

"If you have, it won't be a tragedy. You and your lists."

Jesse plopped himself down in the next chair and said, "It's today! Hip hip hooray!"

"Yes it is, Jesse," said Jodi. "Wish me good luck."

"I hope you sell every one of your paintings, Jodi. Every one!"

"Well, that's a lot to wish for, but I hope I do sell a few of them at least."

The Parkers soon arrived at the table, and, of course, that led to Sammy and Jesse planning their day together.

"They will be having fireworks after the barbecue," said Alex. "The inn wasn't serving the nighttime meal because there would be so much food in Windy Point. They always have a great display. You won't want to miss it."

"We are taking the van, so if anyone wants to ride with us, there will be room," said Susan. "The barbecue starts around six o'clock."

"Jodi, you and I should leave here before eight o'clock this morning to get you all set up for the gallery," said Dad.

"I'm ready, Dad. All my paintings are already packed in the truck, and I just have to tie up one or two loose ends."

"Another list to complete," whispered Susan to her husband.

They gave each other a knowing look that said they loved their daughter anyway.

◊◊◊

As Jodi and her dad rode into town, they chatted about the different events at the celebration.

"I know the Windy Point High School Band is going to be playing patriotic songs," said Jodi, "and Trisha Nevins will be singing the National Anthem. She has such a pretty voice."

"Mobley's is selling raffle tickets for some really nice prizes," said Dad. "The Adams are cooking the barbecue, so we know that will be fabulous. I think I heard that Sam Jackson down at the docks would be giving boat cruises along the coastline. Plus, the Sack & Go is doing a dunking booth with Billy Joe Stickley in it. That's probably the most movement they will get out of him all summer."

"*And*, of course, we will have some of the locals jamming with their instruments playing who knows what!" Jodi said.

"*And* don't forget that local artist who will be doing her first showing in Windy Point!" Dad laughed.

"Now I am really getting nervous," said Jodi.

The trailer was parked along the row where Jodi was to set up her display. The white lattice looked great. Mom's banner was so bright and colorful that it was sure to draw attention to her booth. Dad had attached the tarp overhead so the bright sunshine wouldn't be on Jodi or her work. She and Mandy, who had promised to help her set up, had just finished hanging the last of the paintings.

"Wow! Just wow!" said Mandy. "It couldn't look any better, Jodi."

"You are such a great friend, Mandy," said Jodi. "You have helped me so much with all this."

"When you go off to school this fall, don't forget where you left me," Mandy said.

"Oh, how could I ever forget *you*?" Jodi replied.

"Don't make me cry, Jodi. I really will miss you when you leave."

"We will always be best friends, Mandy. Always. Besides, where else would I get such great barbecue?"

Jodi laughed, and they hugged each other as Mandy dried her tears.

Chapter 9

Fourth of July

It was ten o'clock, and the event was about to start. People had been milling around even before then, waiting to enter the event area. Now, there was a trickle of people going from booth to booth checking out what was there. Most of the people Jodi saw were from Windy Point or the surrounding areas, but there were also quite a few strangers browsing the booths.

"Hey, Jodi!"

Jodi turned to see Pam, an older girl from one of her classes in high school. She'd been away at college this past year but must have come home for the holiday.

"How is school going?" Jodi asked.

"It's good but kind of hard," Pam replied. "I hear you are leaving this fall to go to Atlanta."

"That's true. I'm going to The Atlanta School of the Arts."

"Judging by your paintings, it looks as though you've already been there," Pam said.

"Well thank you, but I still have a lot to learn."

Pam leaned a little closer to one of the paintings. "Isn't that the shoreline along the lower reef?"

"Yes, it is. I'm glad you recognized it."

"I love that spot. Whenever I have a problem, I always go there to think it through. I would love to have that painting to take back to school with me. I'm sure it would help me when I am down. You did a beautiful job with the colors and the light on the water, Jodi. I'll take it."

Jodi smiled and put the painting into a bag for her. "You are my very first sale, Pam," she said. "Thank you so much."

"No, thank *you*," Pam told her. "It will be great to have a piece of Windy Point to take back to school with me."

By eleven o'clock, Jodi had several people crowding around her booth admiring her paintings.

"And just who is this artist?" asked an older gentleman who had been looking for quite a while.

"I am," replied Jodi. "I'm Jodi Bennett."

"You?" he said. "One so young? How can this be? Some people train for years and aren't this good."

"Well, I will be attending art school in the fall," she told him.

"I am very impressed, young lady. I would like to enter some of your work in my next showing. Would you be interested?"

"I—I don't know . . ." she stammered.

Just then, Jack Parker walked over with Sammy. "Jodi, is this gentleman interested in showing your work?"

"Yes, he is, but I don't know . . ."

"My name is Jack Parker, sir," he said. "I own and operate the Parker Art Gallery in New York. I'm staying at the Inn that Miss Bennett's parents own. And who might you be?"

"My name is Peter Maxwell. I have been an art teacher for over twenty years, and I own a gallery in Atlanta called the Artist's Eye."

"I've heard of your gallery, Mr. Maxwell," said Mr. Parker. "Miss Bennett here is very talented but also a little inexperienced in how to handle her work. I'm sure you understand."

"Yes, I surely do understand. Perhaps I could have the opportunity to speak with your parents about this. Would you like that? And you, Mr. Parker, you could be there too, if you wish. Here is my card, Miss Bennett. I will be in Windy Point until next Friday. Discuss this with your parents and, of course, Mr. Parker, and let me know what you decide."

"That would be fine Mr. Maxwell," said Jodi. "Thank you very much."

Jodi watched Mr. Maxwell walk away. She looked down at his card in her hand.

"Do you believe me now, Jodi?" Mr. Parker said and winked at her.

"I'm beginning to, Mr. Parker. It's just so surprising to me that people are interested."

She tried to settle herself so that she could tend to her other customers. Mrs. Mobley had just spoken to her about the painting with the children at the water's edge.

"Do you know that these two are the perfect image of my two grandchildren? I recognized them the minute I saw them. I have to own this one, Jodi."

"It would be my pleasure, Miss Martha," she said as she slipped the painting into a bag for her.

Another lady Jodi did not recognize was holding an ocean scene that she was admiring.

"This one exactly matches the colors in my office," she said. "It's perfect and just the right size, too. And that one over there—the one with the sunset. That would be a perfect match. I'll take them both."

All Jodi could think of was what Jesse had said early that morning: *It's today! Hip hip hooray!*

Mom and Dad came by the booth.

"How are you doing so far?" asked Dad.

"Doing?" said Jodi. "How am I doing? I'm doing *wonderfully!*"

After explaining her conversation with Mr. Maxwell, she told them about the paintings that Pam, Mrs. Mobley, and the other lady had bought. She was almost weak in the knees.

"That's terrific, Jodi!" said her Mom. "We knew you would do well. We are so proud of you."

Her Dad just stood there and grinned at her. "That's my girl," he said as he gave her a big hug.

Several people came by the booth to stop and admire her work. Some gazed a little more closely and lingered a while longer.

"There is something about your paintings that holds your heart," one woman told her.

"Thank you so much," said Jodi. "I do try to put real life into my work."

"I believe it shows," said the woman. "I just love the expressions on these children. They are so *real*. I want this one with the children in the park. Where did you learn how to paint so well, young lady?"

"It's always been a passion of mine, ever since I was a child," she told her.

"You mean you have never had training?"

"No, but I am taking classes in the fall."

"I want my good friend to see these. She's a decorator. Joyce! Come over here, will you? I think you will be impressed by this young woman's work."

Her friend approached the booth.

"Look at these beautiful paintings," said the first woman. "Aren't they just what you need for your clients?"

"Oh my goodness!" said Joyce. "They are, indeed. I have several clients who own beach homes, and some of these are perfect for that." She looked over the remaining paintings and said, "If I were to take these five, could you give me a small discount?"

"I'm sure we could work out something," Jodi told her.

"Please, take my card and give me a call when you have more to sell, would you please?" said Joyce.

"I would be glad to," said Jodi.

The two women walked away, thrilled with their finds.

◊◊◊

Mr. Parker, Sammy, and Jesse headed over to Mobley's booth, where they had raffle tickets for prizes.

"Look at all the neat stuff!" said Sammy.

"They even have some terrific airplane models to win!" said Jesse.

"I think we might have to buy a couple of tickets, guys," said Mr. Parker. "What do you think?"

"Yeah, yeah. We sure do!"

Mr. Parker bought the boys some tickets and learned that the drawing was to be held just before the barbecue was served.

"I hope you and I win," said Jesse.

"Me too," said Sammy.

"I see some boats, Jesse," Mr. Parker said.

He had told them about the boat cruises Sam Franklin was giving, and, of course, they wanted to go. After paying for their tickets, they all climbed into the big boat. It had a bench seat along both sides and could hold about ten people. Mr. Franklin gave them a nice ride just off-shore so they could see how the town looked from the water. Sammy loved the waves and couldn't stop talking about how they went up and then came back down. They traveled up the coast.

"Hey, that's the Sea Bird!" said Jesse.

"Yes it is, and a pretty bird she is, at that," said Mr. Jackson.

After about fifteen minutes, the boat turned around and came back down the coastline. The kids loved it. They spoke as if they had traveled for hours.

"I want to be the captain of a big boat," said Sammy.

"Well, you just come back when you grow up, and I will teach you how," said Mr. Jackson.

"Thank you, Mr. Jackson!" the boys called as they stepped back onto the dock.

"I'm glad you had a good time," he told them.

"I'm sure they did," replied Jack.

◊◊◊

Susan and Alex walked around looking at the other booths. When they came across the one with the Sac & Go dunking booth, Alex said with a chuckle, "I just have to dunk that man. I want to see if old Stickley can really move."

After he paid for the ticket, he drew back his arm and tossed the ball hard at the circle. He missed, but he still had two more throws. Alex squinted one eye and threw again. Another miss.

"Well, here goes nothing," he called.

He pitched the ball, hit the target, and down went Stickley. *Splash*! He bobbed there looking like a drowned rat.

"That was well worth the cost of that ticket," Alex laughed.

"It's almost six o'clock, and that means barbecue," said Susan. "I bought a raffle ticket. They said the drawing is right before they serve the food."

They decided to walk over to the Mobley's booth to hear who won the raffle prizes. As they approached the booth they saw Jack with Sammy and Jesse in tow.

The first-place ticket drawn was a pressure cooker and was won by Shirley Jackson, the third-grade teacher at Windy Point Elementary School. The second was a set of cookout grill utensils and was won by Harley Smith, who ran the local filling station. Third place was for a set of screwdrivers and was won by Sarah Ashby, the Bennetts' cook.

"Now, ain't that a fine howdy do!" Sarah said.

Fourth place was a model airplane kit won by none other than Sammy Parker.

"I told you I would win!" he said. "I told you! Look, Dad, it's the one I wanted, too."

The very last ticket was also for a model airplane and was won by Mr. Parker.

"I think I gave you the wrong ticket, partner," he said. "This is for you, Jesse."

"Thank you, Mr. Parker!" said Jesse. "That's awesome!"

Both boys headed for the barbecue booth with huge grins on their faces.

"I think they are two happy little boys," said Susan.

"I agree," said Alex. "They are really best buddies."

Chapter 10

It was beginning to get dark, and by now, all of the booths were beginning to close up shop. Jodi had sold all but seven of her paintings.

"I'm *so* happy for you, Jodi!" said Mandy. "I knew you could do it. Those last two ladies were so thrilled with your work."

"Can you believe it? A decorator!" said Jodi.

"And don't forget about Mr. Maxwell and the Artist's Eye," said Mandy.

"I don't know about you, but I am starved," said Jodi. "I need some of your mom's barbecue. Let's go find Mom, Dad, and Jesse and get some."

"I'm way ahead of you!" said Mandy.

The Bennetts were already at the barbecue stand with Jesse and the Parkers. They had just gotten their plates.

"Any left for us?" said Mandy.

"I'm sure there is. Why don't you get a plate and meet us over on our blanket so we can watch the fireworks together? The Parkers and some others will be there too."

"Okay, we'll be right there," said Jodi.

As they were leaving the line, they passed Emily Jenkins who had just bought some homemade saltwater taffy that was made by the Sand Dollar.

"Oh, I see you bought some of our taffy," said Mandy. "It's really yummy. I have a hard time not eating it when we make it."

"It's always been a favorite of mine," said Emily.

"Come join us over there for the fireworks," said Jodi.

"Let me get a drink, and I will be right there," said Emily.

The crowds gathered around the platform where the music would be presented. The school band tuned up their instruments. All the band members had parents and relatives in the audience, and cheers went up after each song played. Now, several of the local musicians came onto the stage. There were two guitars, a fiddle, two banjos, a drummer, and even one guy playing spoons. The crowd stomped their feet and clapped their hands to the music, just trying to keep up.

After that, there was a change of pace. Now Trisha Nevins came on stage. She sang a rendition of the National Anthem that raised goosebumps on many spectators' arms.

"Her voice is beautiful," said Alex.

Everyone agreed. It was the perfect lead-in for the amazing fireworks display. Every time one exploded, the crowd cheered. The children were so excited, and the lights from the flashes reflected back off the water.

"I never get tired of this," said Susan. "They are so beautiful."

"This has been a great summer," replied Alex.

"It really has," she said. "I almost wish our guests didn't have to go back home." She turned to Meredith Parker. "Jesse has loved having such a good playmate. He will really miss Sammy when you leave on Friday."

"We will have Sammy write to Jesse after we get home," said Meredith. "I know they'll want to stay in touch with each other."

"That would be great. We'll swap addresses before you go."

By the time everyone had loaded back into the van, it was almost ten, and the boys looked sleepy.

"Well, I have to tell you how much I enjoyed all of this!" said Miss Jenkins. "Atlanta has lots of entertainment, but it isn't as homey as this. I will most definitely come back again next year."

Robert Kensington told them he had decided that his new book would be written about a small, coastal town in Georgia and its wonderful townspeople. Of course, they all were thrilled to hear that.

"Imagine that!" said Sarah. "Us in print."

They all laughed as they rode back to the Sea Bird.

Chapter 11

It was Monday morning, and most all of the excitement had died down. Everyone talked about how much they had enjoyed the celebration as they gathered around the breakfast table, chit-chatting about their plans for the day. It seemed each would be going their separate ways. Miss Jenkins said that she would be leaving that afternoon.

"I can't tell you all how wonderful this has been for me," she said. "I came from a family where I was an only child, and you all have been like real relatives to me. When I return to Atlanta, I'll miss all this relaxation."

"I'll be sure to go to Atlanta to see that apartment," said Jodi.

"Just give my agent a call and tell her who you are," Miss Jenkins replied. "She will be glad to show it to you."

"I can't wait to see it," said Jodi.

"It was my first apartment when I moved to Atlanta," said Miss Jenkins. "It has great memories for me."

Robert Kensington was going into Windy Point one last time to interview some of the locals for his book.

"If I decide to use this as my book subject," he said, "I will, of course, have to come back to gather more notes to write it."

"Just let us know when you want to return, Mr. Kensington," said Alex. "We will be glad to have a room for you."

"That would be wonderful. The inn would be such a good place to gather what I need for my book."

Jodi's room seemed totally empty, since most of her paintings were now gone. She still had the one of Sammy on the beach that she had yet to finish. She loved this painting.

For some reason, she could not decide what was missing. When she turned away from it, the eyes seemed to follow her. She decided that if she continued to think about it, the missing something might be more apparent. She stood there, looking at it a while longer, then went downstairs.

◊◊◊

Jesse and Sammy walked down the beach collecting shells again. Sammy wanted to find a full, intact starfish to add to his collection before he had to go back home. So far, all the ones they had found had broken pieces.

"I want to find a whole one," he told Jesse.

"Yeah, I know," Jesse said. "We will just have to keep looking. They aren't so easy to find."

They wandered down the beach with Sparky running along behind them. There was a jetty ahead.

"I have found some really neat shells along this one," said Jesse.

Sammy raced up ahead when he caught sight of the jetty. "Just what are these things for, anyway?" he asked Jesse.

"These are called jetties. They keep the water from washing away so much of the beach. They also keep the bigger waves from coming so close to shore. If you get out past the jetties, the waves get bigger."

"I like the big waves," said Sammy.

"Yeah, but if you are swimming, they can get kinda scary," said Jesse.

"I think the big waves would be fun if you were in a boat."

"That depends on how big the boat is."

◊◊◊

At lunch, Alex came in and told Jesse that the two of them were going into town to get a haircut.

"Okay Dad," said Jesse. "I'll be ready whenever you say."

Jodi told her mom that she would be going into town to help Mandy's mom clean up after the barbecue food.

Lunch was rather quiet. Several of the guests were out enjoying their last few trips to the beach or to town. After they had eaten, Susan, Jodi, and Sarah cleared the table. Sarah and Susan would be making apple pies in the afternoon, so they started getting out their supplies in the kitchen. Mr. Parker was going into Windy Point to look for artwork to take back to the gallery in New York. His wife Meredith was in their room writing postcards to their friends back home.

Sammy went out the back door, trying to find something to do. Since Jesse had gone into town, Sparky tagged along with Sammy.

Sparky brought the ball over and dropped it at Sammy's feet.

"I guess you want to play catch, don't you?" said Sammy.

He threw the ball across the yard, and Sparky chased after it. He had to tug at the ball before Sparky would let go.

"Okay, so you want to play rough, huh?"

Sparky growled a little, but Sammy knew he was only playing.

"I wish I had a dog like you," he told Sparky.

He threw the ball as hard as he could, and it sailed through the air and landed close to the house. He walked over to where it lay and spotted the little boat under the porch.

"You know, Sparky, this might be my only chance to have a ride in this neat little boat. We are going home on Friday."

He wondered if he could pull it out by himself. It had a rope tied to the stern, so he gave it a yank. It didn't move. He jerked it a little harder. This time, it moved some. He pulled it from side to side, and it began to ease out from under the porch. He yanked it once more and it began to break free of the firm sand that was holding it. Sparky helped some by pulling on the end of the rope that hung free. Together, they dragged the little boat from under the porch.

"Wow!" said Sammy. "That's so cool!" He turned the boat over and put the two oars inside. "Come on, Sparky. We'll have to hurry before everyone comes back. Let's get it down to the beach."

It wasn't easy, but the two of them dragged the boat over and past the sand dunes. The boat made a trail in the sand as they pulled it. Now, it wasn't that far to the water.

"This will be a piece of cake," Sammy told Sparky.

Sparky's demeanor seemed to change. Instead of following along with Sammy, he ran up the beach and back down again, barking nervously.

"Quiet, Sparky!" said Sammy. "They will hear us."

Sammy waded out into the shallow water, pulling the boat behind him. After he got out where the boat began to float, he tried to climb in, but the boat wasn't cooperating. It kept moving away from him.

"Hold still, you silly boat!"

Finally, he managed to get inside. Since he had never tried to row a boat before, he struggled to get both oars going the right way. He began paddling out a little further. He was still trying to make the oars do what he wanted.

Sparky was barking louder and louder now. The boat bobbed up and down along with the waves. By the time Sammy had figured out how to steer the boat, he was already out past the jetty.

"This is fun!" said Sammy.

He turned and spotted a rapidly approaching swell in the seawater.

"Finally, a big wave! This will be awesome!"

But as the wave got closer, Sammy noticed that the boat was beginning to tilt to one side.

"Oh gosh, it's going to tip over! Maybe if I steer it into the wave that might make it flat again."

He began to work the oars, but it was too late. The boat turned into the wave and flipped upside down. Sammy was thrown out and into the wave. In an instant, all the fun was gone, replaced by panic as Sammy swung his arms, trying to swim, only to realize he couldn't keep himself up in the waves.

"*Help!*" he shouted. He splashed furiously, trying to grab onto the boat, but it had floated away from him. "Sparky! *Get help—!*"

Saltwater entered his mouth, and he swallowed it. The water was over his head now, but no matter how hard he splashed, he couldn't get back to the surface.

◊◊◊

Sparky continued to bark, watching the boat. He couldn't see Sammy anymore. Where was he? Something was wrong. He wished Jesse were here.

Sparky turned and ran back over the dunes towards the house.

◊◊◊

Susan and Sarah were still in the kitchen finishing up the pies when they heard Sparky scratching at the back door. This was odd behavior for what Sparky normally did, so Susan went to see what was the matter.

When she got to the door, Sparky was barking frantically.

"What is it, Sparky? What is it?"

Susan looked around, expecting to see Sammy, but he wasn't there. Sparky ran off, barked, and then ran back. Susan tried to call him into the house, but he repeated the action. Over and over, he did this.

"Something is wrong, I just know it," she said.

Susan ran back inside the house.

"Sarah," she said, "run up and get Meredith. We have to find Sammy."

Sarah ran upstairs and knocked on the Parkers' door.

"Yes?" said Mrs. Parker.

"Mrs. Parker, you'd better come down here," said Sarah. "The dog is carrying on something awful, and Sammy isn't with him."

The color drained from Mrs. Parker's face. Together, they ran downstairs. Without a word, Susan, Meredith, and Sarah all ran outside and around the house, but Sammy was nowhere to be found. Sparky was still barking when Sarah noticed a long drag mark in the sand along the edge of the yard, bordered by little footprints.

"Do you think this was him?" she asked.

"I don't know, but let's follow it," said Susan.

The drag marks led towards the sand dunes. Susan stopped as a thought suddenly occurred to her.

"I want to go and check something," she said.

She ran back up to the house and looked up under the back porch.

"Oh, God!" she breathed. "The little boat!"

Susan ran as fast as she could back to the dunes. By then, Sarah and Meredith were standing on the beach while Sparky barked and ran wildly up and down the beach.

"The boat!" Susan called to them. "He's taken the boat!"

"What? He can hardly swim!" cried Meredith. "It can't be, it just can't—not Sammy!" Meredith cried as she fell to her knees on the beach. "Jack won't ever get over this!"

Meredith's whole body shook with sobs of grief. Sarah tried to calm her while she held her arms around her.

"I think I see the bottom of the boat," said Sarah. "See, out over that big wave?"

"The—the *bottom*?" said Meredith.

"It must have . . . capsized," said Sarah.

"Oh, God, *no!*" shouted Meredith.

"Stay with her, Sarah," said Susan.

She immediately ran back to the house to call for help, but in her heart, she knew it was too late. She could not bear the thought of what this would do to Jesse. Sammy was the closest friend he had ever had. She shook her head, mentally scolding herself. Here she was thinking of her own son when a dear friend may have just lost hers forever.

"911," said the operator. "What is your emergency?"

"We have a small boy missing," said Susan. "We think he took a little boat off the shoreline at the Sea Bird, and we think the boat may have capsized. We don't see him anywhere, but we do see the boat. It's upside down in the water. Please hurry!"

"We'll have someone there as soon as possible," said the operator.

Susan ran back to wait with the others on the beach.

◊◊◊

When Alex and Jesse got home, the rescue squad was already there. There were several people from the squad in the water. Some were in inflatable boats, looking for signs of Sammy.

"What's happened?" Alex cried.

"It's Sammy, Alex," said Susan. "We think he took the boat out, and it capsized."

"Oh, no . . ." he said. "What about Jack? Does he know?"

"Not yet. He hasn't come back to the inn. Meredith is taking it really hard."

"Where is he?" cried Jesse. "Please, Mom! Where's Sammy? I told him we couldn't take the boat. I *told* him! Why? Why did he do it anyway?"

Susan leaned down, and Jesse threw himself into her arms, sobbing into her shoulder.

"I know Jesse, I know," she told him.

Meredith sat on a blanket on the beach, still crying. By now, she knew it had been too long. Any hope she'd had was gone.

Jodi came running over the dunes. "Mom!" she said. "I heard the sirens when I was riding my bike back home. What is it?"

"It's Sammy, Jodi. We think he may have drowned."

"What?" Jodi cried. "Oh, no! How? What happened?"

"The little boat. He took the little boat out by himself."

"Oh Mom, what will this do to Jesse?"

"I know, Jodi. I was thinking the same thing."

All they could do was watch and pray for Sammy.

◊◊◊

Jack Parker came running over the dunes and saw the group standing on the beach. He knew something had happened, but what?

"Jack!" called Alex. "Jack, there's been an accident. It's Sammy. He took the boat out alone and it capsized."

"God!" said Jack. "Oh, God! Not my son! Not Sammy! He's our only child!"

Jack ran to Meredith where they just held each other and sobbed.

"My baby!" cried Meredith. "Sammy!"

◊◊◊

The rescue people had done all they could. Darkness was almost upon them, but they kept searching for Sammy. One of the men walked down the beach, looking out into the water. When he arrived at the jetty, he saw something bobbing up and down in the water.

"I think I may have found something," he called back.

What he saw were Sammy's light blue swim trunks. Each of them hoped it wasn't what they thought it was. They knew it was only wishful thinking.

Chapter 12

The Parkers had expected to leave on Friday, but Sammy's death changed things forever. They would be leaving Wednesday morning instead.

The Bennetts were almost as heartbroken as the Parkers. Everyone at the inn was unusually quiet. It was hard to lose a child, no matter whose child it was.

Jodi knew how much Sammy had loved the water. She knew he'd loved the big waves. He was just a little boy. How could he have known how dangerous they were? It was so hard to think that she would never see that happy little face again. She would never hear his laughter as the water washed over him. She would never see that happy, little boy at the inn again. He was gone.

Jodi knew that it would take a long time for Jesse to move on from this loss. As for the Parkers, they would likely never get over Sammy's death. It would be a hard summer that none of them would forget.

By Monday evening, the body of Sammy Parker had washed up against the jetty just past where they'd seen the boat. The boat floated in the next day.

The Parkers could not believe what was happening to their family. It was supposed to be a vacation. It had been such a happy time there, only to end in such grief. It would be a long trip back to New York.

The other guests at the Sea Bird all gave the Parkers their condolences and wished them a safe trip home. Sammy's body would be shipped home ahead of them by train. They would drive home with nothing to look forward to. It was a dark day for them all.

Jodi found Mr. Parker alone in his room.

"Mr. Parker," she said. "I want to tell you how sorry I am about Sammy. He was a sweet little boy, and we all enjoyed having him here. I also want to tell you how much I appreciate your help with my paintings. If it hadn't been for you, I never would have moved out of my comfort zone."

"Jodi, all you needed was a little more self-confidence," he told her. "You already have the talent. If you ever need my advice on your art, please feel free to call me. You have our number."

"I will do just that," she replied.

Susan and Meredith gave each other a long, sincere hug.

"I am so sorry that you will both have such a sad memory of having stayed here," said Susan. "We wish it could have been a happier time."

"Sammy had had a great time at the Sea Bird," said Jack sadly. "He also made the very best friend he'd ever had while we were here, too." He turned to his wife. "Come on, honey. We have a long drive ahead of us."

"Thank you for opening your home to us," said Meredith. "The Sea Bird is an amazing place. Someday, we may be back to visit."

"We would love to have you and Meredith anytime, Jack," said Alex.

Alex shook Jack's hand as they got into their car. Susan and Jodi waved after them as Jesse and Sparky ran alongside the car, calling goodbye. Sarah stood waving on the porch, tissue in hand, too emotional to come any closer. By the time the car had driven out of the driveway, they all were in tears. It had been a summer that would never be forgotten. The summer when an unforgettable little boy named Sammy came to visit the Sea Bird.

Chapter 13

Jodi had almost forgotten about Mr. Maxwell. With everything else going on at the inn, he had been the last thing on her mind. While in the kitchen helping her mother plan dinner, she said, "What do you think I should do about Mr. Maxwell and his gallery, Mom?"

"How many paintings do you have left from the showing?" Mom asked.

"I have about seven. But I don't think these are my best work."

"Why don't you call him and explain what has happened here and see if he thinks you have enough paintings to work with. Then, if he wants to wait until you have more finished, he can work that out with you."

"Good idea. I'll go call him right now."

Jodi talked with Mr. Maxwell, and they decided that since she would be starting school soon, it would be best to give it a little more time. He assured her that her work would not be forgotten.

"I will add your name to my list of prospective artists to keep checking on," he said. "Whenever you feel you have work that I would like, you just call me."

"Thank you so much, Mr. Maxwell," she said. "I will do that."

"I can tell by your voice that Sammy's death has deeply affected you," said Mr. Maxwell. "It may influence your painting. A little more time will be a good thing for you. I know from experience."

"When I start to school, I will be sure to visit the Artist's Eye. I would like to see some of my competition."

"Competition is what will keep you on your toes."

"I'm sure it will."

"Take your time, Jodi. You have your whole life ahead of you. Your talent will still be there."

"Thank you for understanding, Mr. Maxwell. I do need some time."

She hung up the phone and went back to helping out in the kitchen. She explained to her mother what he had said.

"I believe Mr. Maxwell has your best interests at heart," said Mom. "The gallery will be there for you when you are ready."

"I hope it doesn't take too long before my spirit comes back to me," said Jodi.

Susan hugged her daughter. "I know how you're feeling. We were all touched by Sammy's death."

Chapter 14

Robert Kensington left the Wednesday after the Parkers departed, and a family from Tennessee arrived the same day. They were Thomas and Georgeanne Moore and their daughter, a pretty teenager named Abbey. They arrived just before lunch was to be served.

"Well, this is good timing," said Alex. "I'll take your bags up to your rooms, and lunch will be ready in about twenty minutes." He turned to his son. "Jesse, take Miss Abbey's bag up for her."

"Sure, Dad," said Jesse. "It's not too big for me to carry." He grinned at Abbey.

"Abbey, this is our daughter Jodi," said Susan.

"How old are you, Abbey?" asked Jodi.

"Nineteen," said Abbey. "I'm going to go to Vernier's College in Atlanta this fall."

"Really? I start at the Atlanta School of the Arts this September. What a coincidence!"

"I'm just starting, too. I was supposed to go last year, but I had a bout with mono and had to postpone it for a year."

"Have you found a place to live while you attend school?" asked Jodi.

"Not yet. We are supposed to look around while we're in Georgia."

"We just had a visitor here at the Sea Bird who offered me her apartment in Atlanta, but I haven't seen it yet. Maybe we could go look at it together. It might be a place we could share."

"I'll talk with my parents and see what we can work out," said Abbey.

The girls spent time getting acquainted before lunch. After they all sat down to eat, the new family introduced themselves to the other guests.

"What line of work are you in, Thomas?" asked John Barkley.

"I raise cattle and have a few other side jobs going on. What do you do?"

"I manage a textile mill," said John.

"Abbey, what do you plan to study this fall?" asked Jodi.

"I want to be a teacher," said Abbey.

"We can't have enough good teachers, can we?" said Evelyn.

"Jodi is a very good artist," said John.

"Really? What kind of subjects do you do?" asked Georgeanne.

"I do a lot of seascapes, of course, but my favorite subjects are children."

"She just had her first showing in our local Fourth of July celebration," said Susan. "She did very well."

"Can I see some of your work?" said Abbey.

Jodi explained to her that she had sold most of her work, but she would be glad to show her what was left. After lunch, Jodi cleared the dishes while her mother and Sarah brought out dessert. They were having some of those delicious apple pies that Sarah was so good at making, and the guests all commented on how good everything had tasted.

"I can see why this inn comes so well recommended," remarked Thomas.

"Wait until you see what we are having tonight," said Alex as he nudged John.

"I've gained five pounds since I got here," chuckled John.

"Remember to run on the beach," said Sarah from the kitchen, prompting a good laugh from everyone.

Jodi looked across the table at Jesse who sat nudging his dessert halfheartedly. She could see he needed something to cheer him up. He had gotten so used to having Sammy as a buddy and was having a hard time finding something to do alone.

"Want to walk to town with me?" asked Jodi. "We can take my camera and take some pictures for some new painting subjects."

"Sure, I'll go with you," he said.

"Abbey, would you like to go with us? It's just a short walk."

"Yes, that might be fun. Mom, I'm going into Windy Point with Jodi."

"Okay, dear," said her mother. "Enjoy yourselves."

◊◊◊

Sparky caught up with them not long after they left the house.

"We can walk along the beach and then cut back towards town if you like," said Jodi. "Or, if you would rather, we can take the route along the sidewalk."

"I'd prefer the beach," said Abbey. "This is beautiful."

"I've lived here all my life, and I never get tired of it," Jodi said.

"Jodi paints this all the time," said Jesse. "She really can paint great water. Sometimes it even looks wet." He laughed.

Jesse picked up a stick and tossed it for Sparky. Sparky ran through the edge of the water and caught the stick in the air.

"That's the cutest little dog," Abbey told him.

"He's my best buddy . . . Well, one of them, at least."
Jodi knew what he was thinking.

"Come on, I'll race you two to the jetty!" Jodi called.

She ran up the beach, quickly at first, and then let up just enough to let Jesse win.

"Aw, you beat me!" she said.

Abbey laughed. "It must be fun to have a little brother," she said. She was an only child.

Up ahead, there were some children playing on the beach. Jodi told Jesse to ask them if he could take their picture. They said it was okay, so he took a photo of them building a sandcastle. He gave the camera back to Jodi so he could help them. Jodi snapped several shots of the four of them, and Jesse joined in playing with the kids. It was good to see him smile.

After Jesse had helped them add another tower to the castle, Jodi teased, "Okay, Jesse. We'd better go if we want to be back before dark!"

When they arrived in town, Jodi suggested they go to the Sand Dollar and get an ice cream cone. Of course, Jesse gave his approval on this idea. Sparky found a place outside by the door. When they went inside, Mandy came over to wait on them.

"Hi, Mandy," said Jodi. "This is our new friend Abbey Moore. Abbey, this is Mandy Adams, my best friend."

"Hi there, Abbey," said Mandy. "Where are you from?"

"We live in Tennessee," said Abbey. "We'll be staying here for a week."

"Awesome! I hope you enjoy yourself while you are in Georgia," said Mandy.

"She's going to school in Atlanta this fall. Isn't that terrific?" said Jodi.

"That's great!" said Mandy. "I think Atlanta would be so exciting. Much more exciting than old Windy Point." She pretended to pout.

"Well, then how come everyone wants to come here for vacation?" said Jodi. "You know what they say: 'You don't know what you have until you lose it.'"

"Well . . . yes," said Mandy, "but I would at least like to visit somewhere else."

Jodi looked over at Jesse who had gotten chocolate ice cream on the tip of his nose. Out came the camera to capture this moment. He gave her a big grin and licked the ice cream off with the end of his tongue.

"Bet you can't do that!" he said.

"Hmm, you might be right about that," Jodi said, and she tousled his hair and laughed.

◊◊◊

"Bye, Mandy! Bye, Mrs. Adams!" said Jodi as she, Jesse, and Abbey left the shop and started for home.

Dianne Adams waved to her from the kitchen.

"Nice meeting you, Abbey!" called Mandy.

"Bye-bye," she called back.

Off for home, they went with Sparky bringing up the rear.

"I like this place," said Abbey. "It's a little quaint, but it also has some life to it."

"Yeah, we like it, too," said Jodi. "I'm so excited to go to school next month. I can't wait to live in Atlanta!"

"Me too!" agreed Abbey.

"I wonder if Dad would take us tomorrow to see Miss Jenkins's apartment."

"Do you think he would?" said Abbey.

"I'll ask him as soon as we get home. If he will, I'll call Miss Jenkins's agent and let her know we are coming."

After hearing all of this talk about going away, Jesse felt a little down. He realized that with Jodi gone, that would be just one more person he would miss. Sparky walked over next to him. When Jesse looked down at him, Sparky licked his face.

"I know, Sparky," said Jesse. "You are always here for me, aren't you?"

Chapter 15

When they arrived back at the house, Alex was out in the backyard washing the van.

"Hey, Dad," said Jodi. "What have you got planned for tomorrow?"

He scratched his head a little and then said, "Why? What did you have in mind?"

Alex squirted the water hose at Sparky, Sparky had a ball trying to chase the water as the girls explained their idea to visit the apartment.

"Well, I don't really have anything that can't be put off a day or two," said Alex. "I guess we could do that. Do you think your parents would want to go with us, Abbey?"

"They might," said Abbey. "I'll go ask."

"Jesse, what about you?" asked Jodi. "Do you want to go?"

Jesse looked up at her. She figured that if Jesse could see where she might be living, he wouldn't think it was quite so far away.

"Sure!" said Jesse with a smile.

Thomas and Georgeanne felt that Alex would show good judgment about determining whether the apartment was a good place for two young girls to live. They decided that if the apartment interested them and if Abbey liked it, they would go to see it later. The girls chatted away about what kind of place it might be.

◊◊◊

Alex, Jesse, and the girls all got up early the next day to get ready for their trip to Atlanta. Alex had called the agent about the apartment, who told him that they could see it that afternoon. Susan had cooked them a good breakfast and packed some sandwiches, drinks. and snacks for the ride.

Jesse called, "I've got the front seat beside Dad!"

"Okay," said Jodi. "We'll ride in the second row so Abbey and I can talk."

Mom was going to hold down the fort with Sarah. "Y'all be careful," she said.

"We will, honey," said Alex. "We should be back late this afternoon."

"Bye, Mama and Daddy," said Abbey.

"Tell us all about it when you get back, dear," said Georgeanne.

"I have my camera with me, and I plan to take tons of pictures," said Jodi.

Susan caught hold of Sparky's collar while they loaded into the van. "You can't go this time, Sparky," she said.

He seemed to get the message, and as they drove out of the driveway, he wandered up the steps and lay down on the front porch.

As the van approached the city of Atlanta, Jodi felt the excitement rise within her. She knew this would be a real change in her lifestyle. She had grown up living in a calming, peaceful atmosphere. This world was going to be completely different. She began to feel excited and a little scared at the same time.

"Wow!" said Jesse. "Look at all the traffic! Where is everyone going?"

Dad looked at his GPS and watched for his exit. "This is where we get off," he told them. "We'll turn onto Peachtree Road next. That's where the agent's office is." They drove about four more blocks, and he said, "There it is."

They turned into the parking lot and got out of the van. As they went inside, an older woman approached them.

"I'm Janet Fulton," she said. "Are you the Bennetts?"

"Yes, we are. Alex Bennett. This is my daughter Jodi, my son Jesse, and our friend Abbey."

"You made good time, Alex. How was your trip?"

"It was great. Atlanta is really a busy city."

"Well, if you will come and ride with me, we can drive over to the apartment. Emily has told me so much about you, Jodi. I think you will love this apartment."

"I can't wait to see it," said Jodi.

"Neither can I," said Abbey.

◊◊◊

When they pulled up into the apartment complex, Jodi could see that it was not at all what she had expected. Each unit looked like a small house joined to the next. When they went inside, they could see that although it wasn't a large space, it had real character to it. It had a small but useful kitchen that joined the living area. There were built-in bookcases along one wall with a window in between. The furniture, even though it was not new, looked tasteful and homey.

"There are two bedrooms back here with a bathroom between them," said Mrs. Fulton.

"Look, Abbey, it even has a walk-in closet to share," said Jodi. "And this room has good light for me to paint in."

"Yes, it does," Abbey told her.

"The dining table can double as a desk for you," said Mrs. Fulton. "There is also a small patio in the back."

"I think this might be just the place for you," said Alex. "What about the area, Janet? Is this a safe place for these girls? You know they have never lived away from home before."

"This is a gated area, Alex. No one can come inside without permission. I would be comfortable with my own daughter living here."

"That's good enough for me," said Alex with a grin.

Mrs. Fulton talked with Dad about the price and the distance to both of the girls' schools. It seemed to be a very good location for both of them. While the two of them talked, the girls walked around the place, trying to get a feel for it. Jodi got out her ever-present camera and took pictures of everything. Jesse went outside and looked around.

"Hey, Jodi!" said Jesse. "There is a fountain over there. It even has fish in it!"

"How pretty! Wouldn't that make a nice painting?" Jodi took yet another picture. "I love this place! What do you think about it, Abbey? Do you think we would make good roommates?"

"Yes, I do. I really like you, Jodi, and I think we could have a great place here. I hope Mama and Daddy will agree."

"Tell Miss Jenkins that we will get back in touch with her, Janet," said Alex. "I think we will be renting this place."

"Thank you, Alex. I will call her and let her know that you have seen it and seem to like it."

On the ride home, everyone was talking about the apartment.

"I like that it is a gated complex," said Alex.

"I like the storage and character the place has," said Abbey.

"I like the fact that it has room in the bedroom for me to paint," said Jodi.

"I like the fish!" said Jesse.

"Of course you do, little buddy!" said Alex.

Chapter 16

When they got back home, Susan and Sarah had a nice meal waiting for their arrival.

"Okay, I want to know all about the place," said Mom. "Is it close to your schools? Is it safe? Does it have good storage? Is there room for your easel? Is it clean?"

"Yes, yes, yes, yes, and yes," laughed Jodi. "All of the above."

"It's really a nice little apartment," said Dad. "I think we should take it. What do you think, girls?"

"We love it," said Abbey.

"So do I," said Jesse.

"The fish, right?" she said.

They all got it but Mom who looked a little puzzled.

"Fish?" she said.

"Fish," they all said together and laughed.

"I think we should tell Miss Jenkins we want it, even if Abbey's parents decide against it," said Dad. "Jodi could always get another roommate if she had to."

"I think Abbey is a good choice for a roommate," said Mom. "I really hope they agree to get it."

"So do I. It's also a little gratifying that she is a little older than Jodi, since it is their first time on their own."

After hearing all the news about the apartment and seeing all of Jodi's pictures, the Moores decided that the place would be great for their daughter. Alex called Miss Jenkins and told her that they would sign the papers as soon as she could send them.

Now that Abbey and Jodi were going to be roommates, they couldn't stop talking about "their new place."

"I know the exact bedspread and curtains that I want for my room," said Abbey. "I saw them online yesterday. They are shades of greens and blues."

"Sounds pretty," said Jodi. "I want mine to be warm colors like yellows, oranges, and reds. Looks like you are the water and I am the sun." She laughed.

"I can't wait for school to start," said Abbey.

"Doesn't this make you feel really grown-up?" said Jodi.

"Yes, it does. And living in Atlanta, we will have to *be* grown-up to make it, right?"

"I suppose we will."

◊◊◊

The last two weeks of the summer seemed to fly by. Guests checked in and out of the Sea Bird. The Barkleys went home to Iowa. Abbey and her family had returned to Tennessee and Jodi already missed her. The two of them would be arriving in Atlanta about a week ahead of the opening day of school in order to move into their little apartment. In the meantime, they were counting the days.

"Jodi, I think we need to go into town and get your school clothes bought," said Mom. "We don't have that much time left."

"Do you have time to go today?" Jodi said.

"Sarah has already gotten lunch under control so we can go this morning if you want."

"I'll be ready in about fifteen minutes," Jodi told her.

"Jesse, Dad could use some help out back," said Susan. "He's weeding the flower garden."

"Okay, Mom, just a sec," said Jesse.

◊◊◊

Sparky raced Jesse to the door, and together, they went out into the backyard to see what they could do to help Dad.

"If you do a good job, I will take you into town to check out the neat, new models Mobley's got in," Alex told Jesse.

"You mean it?" Jesse said. His eyes lit up the way they always did when anyone mentioned models. "Yeah, sure!"

"Bring that wheelbarrow over so we can load up these weeds," Dad said.

"Here I come," he said as he rolled it a little crookedly over to his father.

Sparky tried helping by dragging the weeds away but, that wasn't making the humans very happy.

"Here, Sparky. Come take a ride," said Jesse as he loaded up the weeds and the dog and rolled them over to the compost pile behind the shed. "Okay, now jump out, boy!"

Sparky barked happily at Jesse. He jumped out and ran back for more. This was more fun than dragging weeds.

◊◊◊

"Mom, I like this blue outfit over here," said Jodi. "It reminds me of the ocean."

"I think that would be nice, too. Why don't you go try it on?"

They picked out several new tops and four pairs of new jeans.

"I guess you will need new shoes, too," said Mom.

Jodi found a pair, but when she looked at the price she was a little disheartened.

"I want these shoes, but they are a little pricey."

"That's very grown-up of you, Jodi, but you have helped me so much at the Sea Bird this year that you have earned all these things and more."

"Thank you so much. I love you, Mom. You and Dad are doing so much to send me to school. I can't thank you enough."

"We know you will make us proud, Jodi," replied Mom.

"I will surely try," said Jodi.

Chapter 17

Tomorrow was moving day for Jodi. She was packing up her clothes for school. She had gotten so many nice new clothes to take with her, and it had been fun figuring out what matched what.

She stood looking at her easel. Jodi knew she would be taking this and her other painting supplies with her. She was so glad that she would have a place to paint while she was at school. There was a large box of snapshots that she had taken as ideas for subjects to paint.

These are going, too, she thought.

Her eyes fell on the not-quite-finished painting of Sammy. It made her heart hurt just to look at it. She knew she wanted to finish this one.

"I'll take it with me," she said. "Maybe I will figure out just what it needs."

She carefully wrapped it with paper and put it in the box of painting supplies. Even after she put it away, she could still see Sammy staring off at the water. It almost haunted her.

"I never knew how much I cared about that little boy."

She began to realize that she had loved him because Jesse had loved him. It was the fact that she wanted whatever it took to make her brother happy. And Sammy made Jesse happy.

That night, after dinner, Jodi called Abbey, and they had talked for almost an hour about seeing each other the next day. Abbey and her parents would be driving into Atlanta from Tennessee. They would be bringing her things to the apartment. All they would have to do would be to unpack everything and make the apartment their home. They both knew that it would be hard to sleep that night. They were too excited.

◊◊◊

Morning came early, and everyone was helping to load the van.

"Is that everything?" called Dad.

"Yes, I just have this one, little bag to bring down," said Jodi.

Mom would stay at the inn with the guests, and Dad and Jesse would drive Jodi to Atlanta.

"I'm going to really miss you, Mom," said Jodi.

"I know what you mean," Mom told her.

"Don't forget I'll be back at the end of the month," Jodi told her.

"I know, I know, but you know how time can be."

"Remember," Jodi told her. "Every time you miss me, I will be missing you too. When you see Mandy, tell her that I will write to her."

"I will," said Mom. By eight o'clock everything was packed snugly into the van.

"Well Jodi, are you ready?" said Dad. "Come load up, Jesse."

"Here I come. Bye, Mom!" he called.

"I'll see you all when you get back!" called Susan.

"We shouldn't be too late, honey," Alex said as he kissed her.

"Jodi, you be careful, and I love you!" Mom said.

They hugged each other tightly.

"I love you too, Mom."

Sarah stepped over to give Jodi a kiss on the cheek before she broke into tears.

"Bye-bye, Sarah," she said.

Jodi waved all the way down the driveway as they pulled out. This was the beginning of a new life for Jodi. She snapped a picture of Mom as they pulled away. Sarah was reaching into her pocket for her Kleenex.

◊◊◊

When they got to Atlanta, Dad had to go see Mrs. Fulton to get the key to the apartment.

"This is so exciting," said Jodi. "I wonder if Abbey has gotten here yet."

"We'll see in just a few minutes. Here we are. There's the complex."

"They're here!" called Jodi. "That's their car over there."

Abbey and her parents got out of their car and walked over to see them.

"Abbey! How are you?" said Jodi

"I'm fabulous!" she said. "How about you, Jodi? Hi, Jesse!"

While the three parents talked, the girls and Jesse hurried to open up the apartment.

"I have moved into this place over and over in my mind ever since we saw it," said Abbey.

"You too?" said Jodi. "I thought I was a little crazy because I did the same thing."

They laughed together.

"Jesse, go see what Dad wants you to carry in, okay?"

"Sure thing, Sis."

Since the apartment had come furnished, the girls only had their clothing and some personal items to unpack. When they had gotten most everything put away, the girls sat down on the couch.

"I think it looks great," said Abbey. "Don't you, Jodi?"

"Yes, I really love it," Jodi replied.

After they had put up their curtains and made their beds, they stood back to admire their bedrooms.

"Perfect!" they said together.

"We knew we could trust your judgment, Alex," said Georgeanne. "This place is perfect for the girls."

"What do you think about us all going out for an early supper?" asked Alex.

"Good idea," said Thomas. "I think we are all a little tired."

After dinner, the group all relaxed a while back at the apartment.

"Well, girls, I guess we should be on our way," said Dad. "Let me know if you need anything. Make sure you lock the doors up every night."

"Dad, Mom already gave me that drill," said Jodi. "We will be very careful. I promise."

"Abbey, your Mom and I are leaving, too," said Thomas. "We have a long drive home."

"I love you, Mama and Daddy," Abbey told them. "I will call you tomorrow night and let you know how things are going."

"Bye, everyone!" Both the girls called as the two cars pulled out of the complex.

"Tomorrow, we will have to stock up on some food for the fridge," said Abbey.

"Yeah, and we can buy our breakfast at that little grill just down the street from here," said Jodi.

"We are going to be *so* busy this year," said Abbey.

"I know. I'm not sure where to start."

"Let's start by going to bed." laughed Abbey.

"I agree," Jodi said.

It had been a very long day for both of them.

Chapter 18

College Days

The next three days were a little awkward for the girls, because they were still trying to find the things that they had just put away. After a while, things got a little easier, and they began to have a routine of sorts. Abbey had discovered a small grocery store about two blocks away that suited them well. Jodi got a schedule for the buses that ran in their area, and the two of them figured out which bus they each needed to catch for school. At least that wasn't an issue anymore. On Thursday, they would both ride their buses to and from their schools to see how long the rides were. This way, they would know what time they needed to catch the bus in order to be on time for school.

"Are we efficient or what?" said Jodi, and they laughed together.

"Yeah, our parents would be proud," said Abbey.

Both Jodi and Abbey had been raised knowing how to cook, so that wasn't a problem for them. Between the two of them, their meals were going well. It was fun to take turns cooking and learning the other's favorites from home. Since both had been born and raised in the South, their tastes were fairly similar.

Jodi and Abbey were becoming almost as close as sisters. This was special to them because Abbey was an only child, and Jodi had no sister. They started calling each other "my sister from another mister." Of course, when they said this, they had to snicker a little.

Monday morning came, and it was the first day of school for both of them. Abbey had been to her school several months before and had visited campus. She knew where her classes would be. Jodi and her parents had come in March and had toured her school. She had gotten her list of classes when she'd tested out the bus route on Thursday.

The two girls stood at the bus stop, waiting for their respective buses.

"I hope you have a great day today," said Abbey.

"You too," said Jodi.

"I almost wish we were going to the same school," said Abbey.

"I know, but we will be together a lot at the apartment."

Jodi spotted her bus rolling up to the bus stop.

"Here comes my bus," she said. "Bye-bye Abbey!"

"Bye, Jodi!" Abbey called as Jodi boarded the bus. "See you this afternoon."

◊◊◊

"I can't believe I am finally here," said Jodi under her breath as she sat down in her first class.

"What?" said the young man seated next to her.

"Oh," said Jodi. "I just said 'I can't believe I am finally here.' I've just been saving for the longest time to help my folks out with my tuition."

"Yeah, I know what you mean," he said. "I've worked hard to get here too. I'm Dave. Dave Langley. I'm from Savannah."

"Jodi Bennett. I'm from a coastal town, too. Ever hear of Windy Point?"

"I heard a friend of mine say his aunt vacationed there this year."

"My parents run a bed and breakfast there called the Sea Bird and we just had a visitor named Miss Jenkins from Atlanta. As a matter of fact, I am renting her apartment for the school year."

"No kidding? Small world, isn't it?"

The class was beginning, and the two of them settled into their work. The chit-chat would have to wait.

This class was about the subject matter of artwork, and Jodi found it fascinating. She knew her camera had helped her find things to paint that she otherwise never would have considered. It had a way of capturing a moment, a movement, or a fleeting expression. She had learned that the right subject matter was essential to hold the viewer's interest.

After class, she and Dave discussed what they learned.

"What type of art are you into?" he asked.

"Oh, my favorite is doing paintings of children," she said. "I've started carrying my camera with me most of the time. It helps me find things to paint I could have missed."

"That's for sure," said Dave. "I'm into photographic art. I'm a shutterbug." He grinned. "It's amazing how many different ways people depict what they see."

Jodi smiled. It was refreshing to find someone else who was so passionate about their work.

"I can't tell you how many years I have dreamed of becoming a famous artist," she told him.

"I'd just like the chance to show my work to the public," said Dave.

"Oh, I just had my first opportunity to do that," Jodi told him. "As a matter of fact, I was able to sell over thirty of my paintings."

"That's awesome!" Dave replied.

"Well, it was just a local thing for the Fourth of July celebration. I did happen to get the attention of an art dealer from Atlanta who was visiting Windy Point. Peter Maxwell. He runs a gallery called the Artist's Eye here in Atlanta."

"I've been there."

"Have you? What's it like?"

"Well, it's fairly large and pretty well-known here. Maybe I could take you there to see it."

"That would be great, Dave. Maybe sometime next week. This one is a little uncertain for me so far."

The two new friends parted and went on to their next classes. Today was going to be very busy.

◊◊◊

When Jodi got off her bus after school, she looked to see if Abbey's bus was in sight. She decided to wait a few minutes so that they could walk back to the apartment together. She had just gotten comfortable on the bench when the bus arrived.

When Jodi spotted Abbey, they both waved excitedly at each other.

"Well, how was your day, Jodi?" asked Abbey.

"It was awesome! How was yours?" she said.

"I had to refresh my memory a little about the campus, but other than that, I loved it. I have some really good professors."

Jodi told Abbey about meeting Dave and how interested he was in his studies.

"You know how goofy I can be about my art," she said. "Well, it seems he is the same way about his photography."

"Two peas in a pod, huh?" teased Abbey.

"Nothing wrong with that!" replied Jodi as she grinned at her.

When the girls arrived back at the apartment, they put away their books and began discussing what they would have for supper.

"Let's just ring for Sarah," laughed Jodi.

"If it were only that easy," replied Abbey.

"How about hamburgers and French fries?" suggested Jodi. "You cut the fries while I make the burgers."

"Sounds good to me," said Abbey.

After supper, they cleaned up the little kitchen, washed the dishes, and sat down to relax on the couch.

"Almost like home," said Jodi.

"No, not really," said Abbey. "At home, I don't have a sister."

"You know, I am really enjoying having you here with me," Jodi told her.

"I know. It would be really boring if we didn't have someone to talk about our day with."

Chapter 19

After several weeks of classes, Jodi and Abbey had gotten into a real routine. Up at six, dress, cook and eat breakfast, wash dishes, walk to the bus stop, arrive at school by seven fifteen, classes from seven thirty until three thirty, walk to the bus stop, home by four fifteen, supper at six, study from seven to nine, and then what they considered a little goof-off time until bed. It made for a very full day. On Saturday mornings, they went to the nearby laundromat to do their clothes. Saturday afternoons were left for grocery shopping, as needed.

So far, things were working out very well. Abbey went to the nearby library for her studies on Sundays. This left Jodi alone to do some painting, and she enjoyed her quiet time with her paints. The first painting she decided to do was the fountain in their apartment complex. The lighting was good there, so she decided to take a folding chair and a little TV table with her for her paints. After she had gotten her easel adjusted, she started mixing her paints. She lightly sketched her drawing onto her canvas.

She considered the scene. The lessons learned in her first class had taught her to be serious about her subject matter. She wanted to be sure this was a good one to paint.

While she was thinking about this, two small boys came to float little boats in the water.

Now *my subject is right*, she thought.

She mentally took a picture of the children's faces. One little boy was clapping his hands when his boat sailed across the fountain. His expression made the painting come alive. The other little boy was blowing his boat across the water. His eyes lit up when his boat came alongside the other one.

A race, she thought. *How cute.*

74

Stroke by stroke, she painted the water. She showed the ripples made by the fountain. They were like little waves for the boats. She added some sparkle to the water from the dappled sunlight coming through the tree boughs overhead. Now, she painted the curving lines of the fountain itself. It was a beautiful form with branches almost like tree limbs. Some were tall and reached upwards while others seemed to reach outward to the water. The water ran out of the branches in an unusual but effective form.

Now, Jodi painted in the little boys who were the life of this painting. This was the part she enjoyed most. She worked closely on the eyes and the expressions they showed. Her mental snapshot was beginning to show on her canvas. The little boys took their boats out of the water and walked over to Jodi.

"Is that us?" one said.

"Do you think it looks like you?" she asked.

"Yes, and that's Tommy over there," he said. "My boat beat his."

"Well, maybe next time, his will beat yours," she said, trying to make Tommy feel a little better.

"How do you do that?" said Tommy.

"Well, I just keep making brushstrokes until I see my painting come to life on the canvas."

"It looks like fun," said the first boy.

"I have always loved to paint," she told the boys. "Even when I was a little kid like you."

It was time for lunch, so Jodi decided that she would do the finishing touches at home.

"See you later," she told the boys.

They waved as they went back to their apartments carrying their little boats with them.

As Jodi was putting her easel and paint supplies away in her room, the unfinished painting of Sammy caught her eye.

What is *it about this one?* she wondered. *Something just doesn't look finished. I just can't figure out what it is.*

She went into the kitchen to make herself a sandwich.

I wonder if they will teach us in school how to know when a painting is finished, she thought. *This one is haunting me.*

As she sat down with her sandwich, Abbey came in from the library.

"Hey, I was just about to have some lunch," said Jodi. "You take this one and I will make myself another."

"Thanks, Jodi. I'm starved," Abbey told her. "I'm just beginning to make a dent in that report I have been working on."

"Well, I worked on a new painting this morning. It's the fountain in the courtyard out back."

"Really? May I see it?"

"Sure, but it's nowhere near finished."

Jodi went to her room and came back with the painting.

"Oh how nice," Abbey commented. "Look at the boys with their little boats! I love it, Jodi."

"The boys even recognized themselves when they looked at it." Jodi thought for a moment, then said, "Abbey, I want you to look at this other one I have been working on. I just can't finish it. Maybe you can see what is missing."

She brought the painting into the kitchen, and Abbey looked closely at it.

"Jodi, I don't see anything wrong with it," said Abbey. "Why do you feel as though something is missing?"

"I don't really know. It hasn't come to life for me yet."

"You'll figure it out."

◊◊◊

Both Jodi and Abbey called their parents that night to update them on the latest happenings.

"Everything is going great, Mom," said Jodi. "We found a laundromat close by and a little grocery store right around the corner from us. The library is only four blocks away, so that's good for studying, and our buses stop less than a block from here."

"How are your studies going?" Mom asked.

"Oh Mom, I am loving it. The courses are so interesting. I really look forward to seeing what is next."

"We all miss you, Jodi. Jesse has been moping around here since you left."

"Aw. Tell him I miss him too."

"I will, Jodi, and Dad sends his love to you."

"I miss you both, Mom."

"Okay, well, you two get some rest, and I will talk to you again soon, sweetheart."

"Bye-bye, Mom."

Chapter 20

School days were passing by, and Jodi and Abbey were deep into their studies. Jodi had learned many new ways to paint, and she admired her professors immensely. Jodi had waited so long for the opportunity to learn about art. She didn't want to miss anything. She had looked forward to seeing Dave Langley again, but it had been hard to find time. They saw each other briefly on their way to and from classes.

One day, one of her teachers asked his students to bring in something they had painted before attending art school. She talked about this with Abbey and asked her which painting she should take. Abbey told her she thought the one of Sammy was the best choice.

"I'm not sure about that one yet," Jodi replied.

"Well, maybe your teacher can tell you what he thinks is missing."

"Now that's an idea," she said.

She wrapped up the painting and put it into a tote bag for school the next day.

On Friday morning, Jodi left for school carrying her painting with her. She was curious to know what her teacher would say about it. As she headed for her next class, she passed Dave in the hallway.

"Hi there, Jodi. What's that you have there?"

"It's a painting I brought in for Professor Archer to see."

"Mind if I have a look?" he asked.

They walked over to a bench along the wall to open her bag. She carefully unwrapped the painting. There were Sammy's eyes staring up at her. They sent chills down her back.

"I wanted him to see this one because I can't seem to finish it," she explained.

"What do you mean? It's beautiful," he said.

"It hasn't come alive for me yet," she told him. "Do you know how it feels when you look at a subject and something is missing?"

"Yes, I think I know what you mean," he said.

"That's how this painting is for me," she said. "Well, I have to get going so I won't be late."

"Me too. See you after your next class."

Jodi wrapped up the painting and carefully put it back into her bag.

Professor Archer's class was next and she looked forward to showing him her work. In class, the other students took turns showing the professor what they had brought. When Jodi's turn came, she was a little nervous to show him.

"Now this is quite a painting, Miss Bennett," he told her.

"I want it to come alive for me, and somehow, it just doesn't," replied Jodi.

"What do you find wrong with it?" he asked her.

"I can't figure that out, but I do feel as though something is missing."

"And what might that be?"

"I had hoped you might be able to tell me that," she said.

"Miss Bennett I *can't* tell you that. This is *your* vision. Only you can determine that. Only the artist can determine his or her vision."

She would not forget his words. Jodi had always known that her paintings gave her a certain feeling. Now, she was beginning to understand what the professor had told her. It was *her* art. It had to feel right to her. She would have to figure this one out for herself.

Chapter 21

Before they knew it, the end of the month was upon them, and Jodi was packing to go home for the weekend. Her dad was coming on Friday afternoon to pick her up.

"Are you sure you will be okay with me gone?" she asked Abbey.

"Yes, I will be fine, Jodi."

"You know you could come home with me. It's not like we don't have room."

"I know, but it will give me a chance to get some studying done," said Abbey. She was very serious about her studies and was acing every test she took.

"You are going to be a great teacher, Abbey. No one studies harder than you."

"Mama and Daddy expect me to. They worked too hard to send me here for me not to be serious about my studies."

"Well, don't work the whole time I'm gone. You have to save a little time for yourself."

When Alex pulled into the apartment complex on Friday afternoon, Jodi had her bags sitting by the door.

"Hi, Dad. I'm all ready to go," she told him as she opened the door.

"How's my girl?" he asked her.

"I'm great, Dad, but also glad to be going home for a while."

They hugged each other tightly.

"Hey there, Abbey," said Dad. "How's it going?"

"It's good, Mr. Bennett. Jodi and I have been getting along really well."

"Dad, I've been trying to get Abbey to come stay with us for the weekend so she won't be here all alone."

"Sure. That would be fine with us if you want to come, Abbey. I know how it was when I went away to college and couldn't get home as often as I wanted to."

"Are you sure, Mr. Bennett?" said Abbey. "I don't want to be any trouble."

"Trouble? Are you kidding?" laughed Jodi. "Our house is always full of people, Abbey."

"You go and pack your clothes, and I will be glad to wait for you," said Dad.

"Well, it would have been a little too quiet for me without you, Jodi," said Abbey. "Thanks, Mr. Bennett. I won't be but a minute."

She ran into her room and started throwing her clothes into her suitcase. She was back in a flash.

"I'm ready," she said.

"Wow, that was fast," said Dad. "Come on, girls. Load up."

They were halfway back to Windy Point before they could say "mint julep."

◊◊◊

"Hey, Jodi!" yelled Jesse as they pulled in the driveway.

"Hey, Jesse!" Jodi yelled back. She turned to Abbey and said, "So much for quiet."

They looked at each other and laughed.

Mom came running out to the car. "Hi, girls," she said. "Sarah has a great supper waiting for you."

"Oh boy, have we missed Sarah's cooking!" said Jodi.

"That's for sure," said Abbey.

"Well, we sure have missed you," said Mom.

Sarah walked out onto the front porch, wiping her hands on her apron.

"Sarah, we have really missed your meals," said Jodi. "We can cook to survive, but yours is the best."

"Welcome home, Jodi," said Sarah. "You too, Abbey. Good to see you again."

The dinner table was alive with talk. Everyone wanted to know how the girls were, how school was, and how they liked their apartment. Jodi and Abbey felt like they had been away for years, not just a month. There were new guests at the inn whom Jodi hadn't met. A banker from Florida named Albert Hamilton and his wife Mona had gotten in last Friday. There were also the Turners, Mike and Chloe from Delaware, real estate brokers who had arrived that afternoon. Miss Rene Punchard, a retired performer from New York, came in on Thursday morning. The Bennetts explained to the guests that Jodi and Abbey had been away at school, and this was their first trip home.

"Oh, I can imagine how exciting that is," said Mona Hamilton. "When I was away at Vanderbilt, I could not wait to get home." She chuckled. "We all thought we were so grown up until we were there without our mothers for a month!"

"It does tend to make you grow up a little," said Jodi.

"Mr. Hamilton, what line of work are you in?" Miss Punchard asked.

"I'm a retired banker, my dear," he said. "Worked with the bank for almost forty years."

"Now, he just counts money in his sleep," laughed Mona.

"That's funny," said Jesse.

"Yes it is, son," said Mona. "Especially since he has his eyes closed."

Mona winked at her husband. Jodi thought they seemed like good-spirited people.

"And how about you, Miss Punchard?" asked Mona. "What do you do?"

"I worked in Vaudeville for twenty years until I lost my husband," said Miss Punchard. "We were a song and dance team. After he died, I just couldn't do it anymore. I later became a makeup artist at Warner Brothers. I'm retired now."

"How exciting!" said Chloe Turner.

"It was an exciting lifestyle back then, but I sure couldn't keep up with it now," said Miss Punchard. "I came down here to take life a little slower. So far, it's working." She smiled.

"From what we have seen, this inn will do just that," said Mona. "It's one of the most relaxing places we have stayed."

Susan looked at Alex and smiled. It was nice to hear such a kind of compliment about the Sea Bird.

◊◊◊

It was Saturday morning, and the girls were up early. They wanted to squeeze as much time out of the weekend as they could. First thing was to ride the bikes into Windy Point to see Mandy.

"Hey, Mandy!" Jodi called as they entered the Sand Dollar.

"Oh hey, Jodi! I didn't know you were home!" said Mandy. "Gosh, it's good to see you!"

"Hi, Mandy," said Abbey.

"Hey, Abbey. How's the 'roomie' thing going?"

"No problems so far," said Abbey. "We get along great together."

"Does your mom need you this morning?" asked Jodi. "We were wondering if you could hang out with us for a while."

"Let me go ask her. It's been a little slack so far today." Mandy went into the back of the sandwich shop to talk with her mother. A moment later, she was back. "Mom said I could go as long as I am back by lunch," she said as she returned.

"That's great," said Jodi. "That will give us some time to ride bikes on the beach for a while."

"I'll get mine and meet you out front," said Mandy.

The three girls rode down to the beach where the dunes parted, and they headed towards the lower reef. It was a beautiful spot, and Jodi had painted this seascape before. It was the one that her friend Pam had bought at the art showing. It had always been one of Jodi's favorite places.

"We can walk out onto the reef while the tide is out," she told Abbey.

"This is beautiful," said Abbey. "I've never seen anything like this."

"When the tide is in, you won't even know it is here," Jodi told her.

"I come here a lot," said Mandy.

"Look at all the colors," said Abbey.

"That's what I love about it," said Jodi. "See how the sea grasses sway and move to and fro? It has amazing movement. Look at the coral. There are so many different shapes. It's alive, you know."

"The water is so clear here," said Abbey.

"It's like looking into an aquarium, isn't it?" Mandy said.

"This is why we love the ocean so much," said Jodi. "It's always exciting, always changing. My friend Dave at school is taking photography classes. He would love to take pictures here. I'll have to tell him about it. I never get tired of looking at this."

"I'm glad we got to spend some time together, Jodi," said Mandy. "I guess I had better head back to the Dollar. Mom will be looking for me."

"It's been fun learning about this reef, you two," Abbey told them. "Thanks for sharing it with me."

The girls rode back to the Sand Dollar and said goodbye to Mandy. Jodi and Abbey decided to ride through town and down the roadside back to the Sea Bird. Abbey was still taken in by all the quaint little shops along the way.

"Jodi, I have a paper I have to finish up before I go back to school," Abbey told her when they got back home.

"Okay," Jodi said. "I will see if Mom needs any help. If she doesn't, I may work on a new painting."

While Abbey set about working on her paper, Jodi went into the kitchen to talk with her mom and Sarah.

"We're back, Mom. Anything I can do to help?"

"I don't think so, Jodi," said her mom. "We are just finishing up in here."

Jesse came in from the backyard.

"Hey, kiddo," said Jodi. "I'm going down on the beach to paint a little. Want to go with me?"

"Sure thing!" said Jesse. "Wait until I get a bucket. I'll look for shells while you paint."

She went upstairs to get her painting things. When she came back down, Jesse was waiting for her with Sparky wagging his tail beside him.

"You can come too, Sparky," she said as she ruffled the fur on his head. "Mom, Abbey is upstairs doing some homework. We won't be too long."

"Okay, you three have fun."

Together, they went down the front steps and out to the dunes. Jesse was carrying his bucket in one hand and Jodi's paints in the other. She had her folding chair over one arm and her easel under the other.

"Where do you want to set up, Jodi?" Jesse asked.

"Right here would be good," she said as they came down the other side of the dunes. "I want to paint it at a slightly different angle."

Jesse put her paints down and helped her open up the chair. "I'll let you set up the easel because I don't know how you want it," he said.

"That's fine, Jesse. You've already been a big help. Stay between the jetties so I can see you."

"I will, sis," he told her.

Sparky chased after him as he walked down towards the jetty. As she sat looking out at the water, she realized that this was almost the same place on the beach she had been when she had painted Sammy. The painting was burned into her mind so well that she could just see Sammy standing there, overlooking the water.

That poor little boy, she thought. *What have I left out of your painting, Sammy?*

Jesse called over to her. "Look at this neat shell I just found!"

"Cool, Jesse," she told him.

Sparky ran back to see what Jesse had in his hand. He was so much a part of Jesse's life.

A part of his life . . . **she thought.** *A part of his life.*

She stared at the water.

Sparky was a part of Sammy's life, too, while he was here.

She watched Sparky as he ran back and forth chasing the water.

He was there! Sparky was there when it happened! He was always there. Sparky ran to get help. How could I have forgotten that? He watched Sammy go under.

"*That's* what's missing," she whispered. "It's Sparky! I've got to put Sparky into my painting." She was so thrilled that she had discovered the missing element in her work. "Wait until I tell Professor Archer! I'm so glad I finally figured this out for myself. Sparky will complete my vision."

Jodi was too excited to start a new scene. All she could think about was Sammy's painting. She walked down to where Jesse was and helped him look for shells. It was good to spend time together again. She had missed him, too.

Chapter 22

It was Monday morning, and the girls were back in school again. The weekend had gone by all too quickly. Sarah had sent them back with a bag full of goodies she had made to keep them happy.

"We'll have to remember not to eat them up too quickly," said Jodi.

"I know," said Abbey. "We can't cook like Sarah does."

Books and studying became routine again. Classes came and classes went, and together, they were working hard to learn as much as possible. They both took college seriously and felt it was a privilege to be there.

Jodi took every chance she could to set up her easel and work on Sammy's painting. It was as though she needed to make it a priority. She hadn't told Abbey about discovering the missing element in the painting. She wanted to wait until she had finished it. She would show it to her when she felt it was complete.

Today, Jodi only needed a little more time to work on Sparky. She wanted to show that playful side of him. He was never still, so she had to show movement on the canvas.

"That's it," she said. "He's jumping up beside Sammy, trying to see the starfish in his hand, just like he did when Jesse found the shell the other day.

Part of his life . . . **she thought again, sadly.** *Part of his very short life.*

Finally, the painting was finished. Jodi felt as though she had completed a mission assigned to her. She could check this one off her list.

◊◊◊

After class on Tuesday, Dave approached Jodi in the hallway.

"I was wondering if you would be busy this afternoon," he said. "I thought maybe I could take you to the Artist's Eye."

"That would be great. I don't have anything planned for today. I'll call Abbey and let her know I won't be home for a while."

Dave met her at her apartment and together they walked to the gallery.

"We are close to so many things," she said. "I love being able to walk to almost all of them."

"I know what you mean," Dave replied. "It's almost like living in a little town inside a bigger town."

When the two of them walked inside the gallery, Jodi just stood there spellbound.

"This is awesome, Dave," she told him. "I didn't know it would be this big."

"Look over here at this piece," Dave said as he led her across the room to a beautiful black and white photograph of waves rushing against an ocean cliff.

"It's so exciting," she said. "It makes me feel like I am right there on the cliff."

"Yes, it does. I really admire this man's work. He has others here too. Someday, if I am lucky, I want to have some of mine here."

"You should let Mr. Maxwell see some of your work," said Jodi. "I think he would be impressed. Did I tell you that I finally finished Sammy's painting?"

"No, you didn't. I would love to see it," he said.

"When we get back to my place, I will show it to you," said Jodi.

They continued to stroll through the rooms, looking at all of the artwork. There were other pictures of beach scenes and many of similar subjects Jodi had experience painting. One thing she did notice was that not many had children in them. Jodi always felt that people in a painting helped make it come to life. She mentioned this to Dave. He thought for a moment.

"Maybe the 'people part' of your paintings will be what makes yours unique," he said.

"I hope so, because my work doesn't feel finished if I don't add people to it," she said. "Sometimes the missing something isn't just people."

"What do you mean?" Dave asked her.

"You'll see when I show you my painting."

There were so many rooms with paintings, photographs, and sculptures. It was almost impossible to see them all as closely as Jodi would have liked.

"We'll have to come back again to take them all in," said Dave. "Every time I come, I see something different."

"I would like that," she said.

As they walked back to the apartment, Dave took hold of Jodi's hand. She was a little surprised, but it felt right to her. He looked down at her and smiled.

"I'm glad I could bring you here, Jodi," he said. "I knew you would enjoy it."

"I did. I really did. Thank you so much Dave."

He gripped her hand a little tighter and smiled. "We have a lot in common, Jodi. I can see it in your eyes when you look at artwork. You look at it like I do. I knew that the first day I talked with you."

They walked on, chatting about some of the work they had just seen.

When they arrived back at the apartment, Jodi invited Dave in to look at Sammy's painting. She brought it out and unwrapped it.

"Can you see what is different?" she asked.

He studied it for a moment. "The little dog. He looks really lively."

"That's my brother Jesse's dog, Sparky. Sparky was always following Sammy while he was at our inn. He was with him when the boat capsized. He ran for help when Sammy drowned. Sparky was the missing element. I don't know why I hadn't thought of adding him before. You know, every time I looked at this painting, it was if Sammy himself were trying to tell me something. It was in his eyes. Now, I feel good about this painting."

"I can see that, Jodi. You look like you just found the missing link. I really like this one. His eyes tell so much. And the little dog—his movement is awesome. He looks as though he could jump off the canvas."

He grinned at her, and she laughed.

"He probably could," Jodi said. "He's never still."

Chapter 23

The trees in Atlanta were changing colors, and Jodi took advantage of this by capturing some of the scenery on canvas.

By now, she had completed several more paintings. These were such different scenes from what she normally painted. There was one of children playing in the leaves. They were throwing them over their heads and laughing. One showed a young woman reading in the park while the leaves slowly fell around her. Jodi loved working in all these warm colors. It was so different from the beach scenes she usually did, which were mostly greens and blues.

One day, Dave drove her out to a nearby farm that raised horses. Of course, she took her camera with her. She took a beautiful photograph of the horses running in the meadow. Gorgeous trees surrounded it and provided a glorious fall backdrop.

"This is awesome, Dave," she said.

"You have a great eye for subject matter, Jodi," he told her.

"My professors have helped me with that," she said.

Together, they walked through the trees along the meadow. Dave had his camera, too, and they took several shots along the way.

"This is my uncle's place," he told her. "I used to come here during the summers when I was a kid. It's part of the reason I wanted to do photography. I couldn't get enough of this scenery. I wanted to take it home with me." He laughed. "My Uncle Jack bought me my first camera so I could do that. I've loved it ever since."

"That's almost like me. I've always known I wanted to paint, ever since I was a little girl."

"Addicted since birth, huh?" he laughed.

◊◊◊

Since Jodi had finished several more paintings, she thought again about contacting Mr. Maxwell at the gallery. She decided to call him and see if he wanted to see her work again.

"The Artist's Eye, Peter Maxwell," he answered.

"Mr. Maxwell, this is Jodi Bennett from Windy Point," said Jodi. "I was wondering if you would have time to look at some of my newer paintings."

"Jodi! I certainly would. When can you bring them in?"

"I'm here in Atlanta attending school, so I could come most any afternoon that would suit you."

"What about Thursday, about four-thirty?"

"I can do that," Jodi said.

"I will see you then," said Mr. Maxwell.

Wednesday at school, she looked for Dave. She finally spotted him in the cafeteria at lunch.

"Dave, I need a favor from you," she said.

"Sure! What do you need?" he asked.

"Are you doing anything at about four tomorrow?"

"No. What gives?"

"I have an appointment with Mr. Maxwell at the gallery, and I need help carrying my paintings there."

"You talked to him! Great! Sure. I'd be glad to help you. I'm excited for you, Jodi."

◊◊◊

The next day, Dave met her at the apartment. They got all of her paintings together and wrapped them. She had borrowed a small cart to get them to the gallery, and they walked the few blocks to the Artist's Eye.

"This is awesome for you, Jodi," said Dave. "I hope he appreciates your work as much as I do."

"I want you to talk to him, Dave. He should see your work, too."

"This is about you today, Jodi," he said. "My work can come later."

Mr. Maxwell was in his office and welcomed them in pleasantly.

"It's good to see you, Jodi!" he said. "I was hoping to see your work again."

"It's good to see you too, Mr. Maxwell. This is my friend Dave Langley. He's come to help me today."

"Hello, Dave. Nice to meet you as well."

"Thank you, Mr. Maxwell," said Dave. "I've been to your gallery several times and always want to come back again. I am attending the same school as Jodi. I'm studying to become a photographer."

"Wonderful! We can never have enough art," Mr. Maxwell replied. "Well, Jodi, let's see what you have here."

He had a large table set up for her artwork. They unwrapped her paintings and laid them out on the table.

"I like what I see," he said. "These are very good, Jodi. I am impressed with your use of colors, and, of course, I love the children you put in the picture." He gestured to the painting of Sammy and Sparky. "This one with the boy on the beach is especially good."

"That one is very dear to me," said Jodi. "He's a little boy who stayed at the inn last summer."

"He's the one who drowned, isn't he?" asked Mr. Maxwell. "I recognized him right away."

"Yes, it is. I call it *Sammy's Painting*."

"It's very good, Jodi. You really captured him, and, of course, the little dog completes it."

For the next few minutes, they discussed how he would show her work and what kind of prices she could expect to ask.

"I can't believe I will have my work in a real gallery," Jodi said.

"Your work is very unusual, Jodi," said Mr. Maxwell. "I think you will do well. I saw that talent when I was in Windy Point. If anything, you have gotten better. I will be calling you to let you know how it's going."

"Thank you, Mr. Maxwell. I'll be waiting to hear from you."

When they got outside the office, Dave turned to her and gave her a big hug.

"I'm so happy for you, Jodi!" he told her.

"Thanks for helping me, Dave," Jodi told him.

He gave her a big wink. "No problem for my girl."

"Hmm," she said. "I like the sound of that."

Chapter 24

Over the next few months, Dave and Jodi spent time together whenever they could. They always made a point to call each other to catch up on what the other had been doing.

"I really like this guy," she told Abbey. "We are so much alike with our interests. I feel like he knows me really well."

"He is a nice person," Abbey told her. "I like him too."

"His photographs are fabulous. I told him that he should take some to Mr. Maxwell's gallery. I know he would appreciate his work."

Not long after Jodi's visit to the Artist's Eye, Peter Maxwell called to say her paintings were causing some interest.

"I could use a few more, when you have the chance," he told her.

"I'll see what I can do," she replied.

She had started on a couple of new ones, but they were still in the beginning stages. She would have to work them in when she had time between school work.

"I want to finish the one with the little girl and the puppy in the grass," Jodi told Abbey.

"She's so cute and natural," said Abbey. "I like how the puppy is licking her face. It's exactly how puppies and kids interact."

"That's just what I want to catch. The natural part of life."

◊◊◊

Thanksgiving was almost upon them, and Jodi and Abbey's schools would excuse students for a week-long vacation. Abbey would be spending time with her family in Tennessee. She had only been home once since she started school, and it wasn't easy for her parents to drive down to get her because of the farm. It also wasn't easy to get someone to help out while they were gone. She knew her grandparents would be at her house as well. She was packing her suitcase when Jodi came in, excited that she would soon see them all.

"Getting everything ready to go?" Jodi asked.

"Yep! I'm almost finished," said Abbey. "I always pack like I am moving."

"So do I," answered Jodi. "Dad will be here around lunch time. I can't wait to taste Sarah's roast turkey and dressing."

"*Oh, stop!*" said Abbey. "You're making my mouth water."

"I'll probably come back five pounds heavier than when I left," Jodi laughed.

"With your figure, you won't need to worry," said Abbey. "You always look great. Dave seems to think so, too." Abbey winked at her.

"I'm sure going to miss him," Jodi said, frowning.

"You can still talk to him on the phone," Abbey reminded her.

"I know, but it's not the same as seeing those big, brown eyes of his."

"Well, at least you have some big, brown eyes to look into," said Abbey regretfully.

"Oh, listen to you. You know the guys look at you. You'll find someone. Just wait."

Abbey's parents arrived at about eleven o'clock, and not long after Abbey left, Jodi's Dad arrived.

"Look at you!" Dad told her. "You are becoming a young woman, Jodi. Somehow, I never noticed it so much when you were still at home."

"It had to happen sooner or later," she laughed.

"Wait until Mom sees you."

"Dad, I think Mom had a clue," she chuckled.

"You know daddies don't want to see their little girls grow up."

"We can't stay little forever." A thought crossed her mind. "Unless you are someone like Sammy. Someone who was taken before he grew up. It's like he's frozen in time, isn't it?" She sighed.

"I know, Jodi. I think about Sammy a lot. It was such a tragic thing to happen on a vacation. Jack and Meredith were just devastated. I'm sure this holiday season will be hard for them."

"Well, I didn't mean to start out on such a sad note," said Jodi. "Let's get going. My things are all ready."

"Load up, then."

◊◊◊

The Sea Bird was decorated with colorful, dried leaves in large pots on the front porch. Susan had scattered small pumpkins and gourds on the dining table, and there were tall candles in the center decoration.

The inn was alive with people. The Bennetts always booked guests for the holiday, but they also had Susan's parents and her brother staying with them. Jodi and Jesse hadn't seen their grandparents in almost a year. George and Olive Gardner lived in Florida and didn't drive much anymore. Susan's brother Frank had driven them up.

"Well, look at this beautiful young woman!" said Grandpa Gardner. "What have you done with our little granddaughter, Jodi?" He winked.

"I left her on the beach with her little sand bucket," Jodi teased back and gave him a big hug. Jodi spotted Olive across the room. "Hey there, Grandma Gardner. I'm so glad Uncle Frank could drive you up."

"So are we, Jodi." She leaned closer and whispered, "Grandpa just doesn't see like he used to. I would have been a nervous wreck."

"Well, now you are safely here. That's all that counts."

Mom and Sarah had already been cooking up desserts for the feast two days before. You could smell the cakes and pies all over the house.

"Jodi! Mom let me help sprinkle the pecans on top of the pumpkin pies!" said Jesse.

"You did?" said Jodi. "I'll bet they taste delicious. Pumpkin is my favorite."

"*Everything is my favorite,*" said Uncle Frank.

"I'm with you, Frank," said Alex.

"Me too!" said Jesse. "My stomach can't wait."

The Sea Bird was aglow with the candles Susan had just finished lighting.

"The table looks beautiful!" said Olive.

"It certainly does," said one of the new guests. Joshua Turner, a retired businessman, had come down from Virginia to visit with family in Florida. He had decided to make a layover in Windy Point and continue on the following Monday. "They will have such a crowd today, they won't miss old Uncle Josh at all," he laughed. "This looks like a fine group to spend the holiday with, anyway. My family will probably all go out to a restaurant to eat." He caught sight of Sarah's beautifully browned turkey and added, "I think this looks much better."

Another couple had arrived yesterday from South Carolina. Chip and Jenny Waters were college students and newlyweds, and this was their honeymoon.

"Oh! What a terrific way to spend your first married days together," said Olive. "This place can be so romantic. Wait until you take a walk on the beach and watch the sunset. It's glorious!"

"We've heard a lot about this place from friends," said Jenny.

"We will be glad to fix you a private dinner for two by candlelight in your room, if you like," said Susan. "Just let us know when."

"We would enjoy that," said Chip, winking at Jenny.

Everyone sat holding hands together, and Alex said a Thanksgiving Blessing over the food. The meal began. Bowls were passed, glasses refilled, and seconds and even thirds were eaten.

"That was one of the most scrumptious meals I have ever eaten," said Joshua Turner.

"Thank you, Mr. Turner," said Susan. "You have our cook Sarah to thank for this meal."

"Is this lady single?" chuckled Mr. Turner.

"Yes, she is, but you would have to discuss that with Sarah," she said with a smile.

Sarah called from the kitchen, "I heard that!"

Everyone laughed.

Sarah came out carrying another plate. "Have some more pie, Mr. Turner," she said, and she winked and returned to the kitchen.

After dinner, the Bennetts finally got a chance to sit down and have a good visit with Jodi.

"Mom, have I told you I took some of my paintings to Peter Maxwell's gallery?" she asked.

"I knew you had talked with him about it, but I didn't know you had taken any to him," Mom replied.

"I took about eight in, and so far, he has sold three of them."

"That's great, Jodi. Are you still painting?" Dad asked.

"Yes, as often as I can. School keeps me really busy, but I try to squeeze in some painting time. Dave took me out to his uncle's farm and I took pictures of the horses in the fall leaves. I took two works from those photos to the gallery."

"Who is Dave?" asked Dad.

"Oh, haven't I told you about Dave?" she said.

"*No . . .*" **said Dad. "You didn't."** He smiled at her.

"Dave Langley," said Jodi. "I met him on the first day of school. He's taking photography classes. Mom, you would love him. He's *so* into his art. He loves it the way I love painting. He took me to the gallery, and, Dad, it was awesome! They have paintings and sculptures and photography. There was so much to see. I want to go back again. And now, I have my own work there! I can't get used to that idea."

"Jodi, we are so glad we were able to send you to this school," said Mom. We knew you would love it."

"Oh, I do Mom. I do."

After Jodi had gone up to her room, her phone rang. It was Dave.

"Hello, sweetie, how are you?" he asked.

"Hey there, Dave. I was good, but now I am much better. I've missed seeing you."

"I've really missed you too, Jodi. It's just not the same without you around."

"Are you going to Savannah during the holiday?" she asked.

"That's where I am now. You know how you were about that painting? How you felt that something was missing?"

"Yeah," she said.

"Well, *you* are missing . . ."

She smiled. "That's sweet, Dave."

"I didn't realize how much I had you on my mind."

"That's '*Georgia* On My Mind,'" she teased. "Not Jodi."

"Silly girl," he quipped. "At least we're still in the same state."

"True," she said.

"I'm coming back on Saturday. Maybe we can see each other on Saturday night or maybe Sunday if you are back by then."

"I'll call you when I get back to Atlanta," said Jodi.

"I can't wait to see you again, Jodi. Sleep tight. I'll see you soon. Bye-bye."

"Bye, Dave."

Jodi did sleep well that night. It was good to know that the two of them would be together soon.

Chapter 25

When Abbey and Jodi reunited, they talked forever.

"Where did you go? What did you do? Did you have a good time? Did Dave call you while you were gone?"

They had enjoyed the time they had spent with their families. It was a little strange, but the apartment was feeling like home to them now.

Abbey said, "I think I will be glad to get back to my school work."

"I know," said Jodi. "It's like waiting to open a Christmas present. I want to know what school has for me next. I need to call Dave and let him know I'm back. Abbey, I've never felt this way about a boy before. I thought about him the whole time I was at home."

"It must be love!" laughed Abbey.

"I don't know. I've never been in love before," said Jodi, blushing a little.

"Oh, you will know when it happens," said Abbey.

Later, Dave came by the apartment. and he and Jodi got a quick bite at the cafe down the street.

"Want to see a movie?" he asked.

"No, not really," said Jodi. "I just want to spend time with you. It seems like weeks since we were together."

"Yeah, it sure does," he told her.

After walking a few blocks down the street, he took her hand again.

"You know Jodi," he said, "I don't see any other girls. You are the only one I think about. What would you think if I asked you to go steady with me?"

She stopped on the sidewalk and turned her face up to his. "I think I would like that very much, Dave. I really care about you. You were on my mind the whole time I was at Windy Point."

Dave bent down and kissed her on the lips.

"I've fallen in love with you, Jodi," he said.

"I love you too, Dave. I've never felt this way about anyone before."

He hugged her closely, saying, "I hope we don't have to be apart anymore. It was really hard for me."

They walked hand in hand down the street, looking at each other often. Dave stopped a few times to kiss her again.

"Where have you been all my life?" he laughed.

"Waiting for you," she said. "Waiting for just the right guy to come along."

◊◊◊

Abbey spent the afternoon at the library. She had another report that was due in a week or two. As she browsed through the books, she noticed a boy she had seen before.

"I see you are back again," he commented. "I see you in here fairly often."

"I study here a lot for school," she told him. She sat down at the table and began spreading out her papers and books.

"My name is John Forester," he said. "Haven't I seen you at Vernier?"

"I'm a freshman there," she said. "Are you a student there, too?"

"Sophomore year for me," he said.

"I'd be a sophomore too if mono hadn't kept me from starting last year when I wanted to."

"That would be tough. With all this studying you do, I would bet you will make a really good teacher."

"Thank you. What is your favorite course?"

"I love history. I could dig around in that for ages," John told her.

"I like math," Abbey said.

"Whoa! You have to be smart for that!"

"By the way," she said, "my name is Abbey Moore."

"Glad to make your acquaintance, Miss Moore," he said, grinning.

After getting through the first moments of shyness, Abbey began to chat easily with John. Before it was time to go, each had shared a lot about themselves. John had lived in Atlanta all of his life. His father had died when he was twelve, and his mother had raised John and his two sisters by herself. John had worked part-time all through high school just to help make ends meet. He was very fortunate to earn a full scholarship through college, and his mother was so proud of him. Now, it was his dream to teach inner-city children. He knew how difficult it was to be raised with such a hard background.

Abbey explained how her parents ran a farm and how sometimes the crops didn't come in like they hoped or the cattle prices would drop. Both of them knew that college was a gift they couldn't afford to waste.

"Would you like to go out sometime?" John asked. "I know you are busy, but you could name the time and place."

Abbey hadn't been on many dates and was a little unsure of herself. "Maybe we could have coffee at the cafe down the street sometime. Would that be okay?"

"That would be fine. Is tomorrow too soon?" he said.

"I think I could do that. Is two o'clock all right?"

"I can pick you up at your place if you like."

Abbey gave him her address as they said their goodbyes.

"See you tomorrow," he said as he walked down the street.

◊◊◊

When Abbey got home, she couldn't wait to tell Jodi about her new friend.

"I told you that you would find someone," Jodi said.

"Actually, he found me," said Abbey. "He told me he had seen me in school. I've been seeing him at the library too, but we never spoke."

"See how things just work out for you?" Jodi said. "You are such a cute girl, Abbey. It was only a matter of time." She smiled at Abbey.

"Thanks, Jodi. You are a good friend."

Chapter 26

Months had passed, and Christmas had come and gone. Dave and Jodi had grown even closer. They spent time together whenever they could but now, Jodi was busy studying for her finals. If everything went as planned, she would be graduating soon. It was an exciting time for her.

The phone rang as she came into the apartment. It was Mr. Maxwell.

"Mr. Maxwell," said Jodi. "It's good to hear from you. Do you have any news for me?"

"I sure do, Jodi. I've sold several more paintings and was wondering when you can have some more for me."

Jodi had already received money for the others he had sold and had opened a new savings account to deposit the checks. Her paintings had caused quite a stir at the Artist's Eye. People commented on the impressive talent of this new artist, and many had talked about her way of showing the children in her paintings. They were impressed with the expressions and movement she had shown on canvas. One gallery owner had been very impressed and had bought several to take back home. When Mr. Maxwell told Jodi about this, she was surprised that her art would travel like that.

"We never know where your art can end up, Jodi," he said. "People buy, their tastes change, and they also resell, so it could end up anywhere."

She thought about this for a while and commented, "I hope they all find good homes."

"I'm sure they will, Jodi. They begin to feel like part of you, don't they?"

"Yes, they do. Certain ones more-so than others."

She sighed. It was a bittersweet feeling.

She explained to him about her final exams and how much she had to do to be ready for them.

"I understand, Jodi," he said. "We don't want to hinder your studies, do we? You just do what you can. I will just have to be patient and wait. Give me a call when you have a few ready."

"I will, Mr. Maxwell. As soon as I can."

◊◊◊

Dave and Jodi were spending more and more time together now. They knew that once school ended, they would be miles apart again.

"I can't stand the thought of being away from you," he told her.

"Why don't you come to Windy Point and visit when school is out?" Jodi suggested.

"That would take money, Jodi. I will have to find a job to support myself. It won't be easy to start with."

"I'm sure you could find something in Windy Point. Dad might even have enough work at the inn to keep you busy. Keep it in mind, will you?"

"I have some time before graduation. I'll think about it."

"In the meantime, I'll talk to Dad and see what he says. Besides, there are some awesome places for you to take pictures. Maybe you could do photography work there."

"You are making it more and more tempting, Jodi." He smiled at her and kissed her on the cheek.

The girls were spending almost all of their free time working on their studies. It didn't leave much time for either of them to spend with the boys. Of course, the boys were going through the same thing, so it was completely understood. They all spoke when they could find the time, but there was hardly ever enough time to go out.

◊◊◊

On the first day of final exams, everyone was stressed out a bit. Abbey and Jodi said goodbye at the bus stop and wished each other luck.

"Don't worry, Abbey. You will ace them all for sure," said Jodi.

"You too, Jodi. See you this afternoon."

The next day, they could not wait to receive their grades. When Jodi saw the board, she inched closer to look. She was seeing lots of assorted expressions on the faces of those ahead of her. She spotted her name.

Jodi smiled. She had done well on all of her exams. The strain was finally over. It couldn't have been a better day. Later, she waited at the bus stop for Abbey so they could walk home together.

Here she comes, she thought. *I can tell by her face that it was a piece of cake for her.*

Abbey was beaming. "I did it! I did it!" she said. "I passed everything!"

They gave each other a big hug.

"And you were surprised by that?" teased Jodi.

"Now we can both breathe," said Abbey.

Together, they almost skipped home like two little girls. It was a great day for both of them.

Jodi couldn't wait to get in touch with Dave about her exams. When she finally talked with him, they were both excited to tell each other how they had done. Since both of them had taken a one-year course, all that remained was graduation. Abbey, of course, would have three more years to complete. Jodi would miss being with her. They had formed a real bond since becoming roommates. It would be hard to leave her.

Chapter 28

Graduation

Graduation was finally here. The entire Bennett family had come to see Jodi graduate. Sarah would be running the Sea Bird while they were gone.

"I've been doing this since you two were teenagers," Sarah had told Susan and Alex. "If I can't handle it, my name ain't Sarah Ashby!"

Jesse was jumping around almost as much as Sparky. He was so excited to see Jodi. Dave's parents had come up from Savannah to see him graduate. Jodi introduced Dave to her family.

"Mom and Dad, this is Dave Langley," Jodi said.

"Nice to finally meet you, Dave," said Mom. "We've certainly heard a lot about you."

Dad was shaking his hand. "Dave, have you been taking care of my girl?" he said.

"Well, I've been thinking of her as *my* girl," said Dave, "but yes, I have." Dave grinned and turned to his parents. "These are my parents. Mom, Dad, this is Mr. and Mrs. Bennett."

"Well, hello there," said Mr. Langley. "Dave has spoken highly of your daughter, sir. It's good to finally meet her."

"Susan and Alex Bennett, sir," said Dad.

"This is my wife Patricia, and they call me 'Big Dave,'" said Mr. Langley.

"Dave, this is my little brother Jesse," Jodi said as she tousled his hair.

"Hi there, big man," said Dave. "I hear you like putting together models. I did quite a bit of that as a kid."

"Wow! Did you?" said Jesse. "I love working on them, especially airplanes."

"He had models all over his bedroom," remarked Patricia.

"Awesome!" said Jesse. It was clear he liked Dave already.

◊◊◊

When Jodi walked across the stage to receive her diploma, she felt a thrill go through her. Her dream had finally come true. Now, she was on her way to becoming a real artist. The rest would be up to her to make it happen.

Abbey's family had already arrived at the apartment. She and Jodi had both been packing up their things. Abbey would be leaving for Tennessee that afternoon. The Bennetts got there after having lunch out with Jodi after graduation.

"I wish I could have been there to watch," said Abbey. "I know you could only get family tickets."

"I felt you there anyway," said Jodi with a smile. "We've been through all of this together."

"I really hope we can keep in touch with each other after you leave," said Abbey.

"So do I, Abbey. I'm really going to miss you. It's like losing a sister."

"Just think," said Georgeanne Moore. "If we hadn't come to the Sea Bird, you probably would have never met."

"Thank goodness for the Sea Bird," said Jodi.

"I'm going to miss this little apartment," said Abbey."

"Maybe we can rent it for you again next year, dear," said Thomas Moore.

"I sure hope so," said Abbey.

Both families loaded up their daughters' belongings and got ready for their trips home.

"I'll take the key back by Miss Jenkins' agent's place," said Dad.

Abbey and Jodi gave each other a long-lasting hug goodbye.

"Write to me, Abbey!" called Jodi.

"I will!" Abbey called back.

The Bennetts pulled out of the parking lot, heading for Windy Point. The Moores began the trip back to Tennessee. The girls waved sadly as they drove away.

Chapter 29

It had been hard to say goodbye to Dave. Jodi knew it would be a while before they would see each other again. She gave him a call as soon as they got back home.

"I miss you already," she told him.

"Me too," Dave replied. "I've been talking with my folks about coming to Windy Point. I will have to see what we can work out."

"The inn is coming into its busy season, so I guess I'll be working here."

◊◊◊

A week had gone by since Jodi had gotten home, and the old routine was starting again. Mom and Dad were back to managing the inn. Sarah had encountered no problems running it while they'd been gone. Of course, they really didn't expect her to have any. They had just wanted to tease her a little.

"Alex, are you going to get the rest of the old shingles repaired today?" Susan said. "We have guests coming in tomorrow."

"Yes, honey," he told her. "I just have to get that ladder a little more stable. I think I will have to buy a new one soon. Ours is almost shot."

"Well, just be careful, Alex."

He went out back to the shed where the ladder was stored and took another look at it.

"Maybe we can get one more use out of you," he told the ladder.

◊◊◊

Sarah and Susan were setting the table for lunch while Alex replaced the shingles above the dining room window. Just as Sarah turned to go back into the kitchen, she thought she saw something flash in front of the window.

"What was that?" she asked Susan.

"I don't know."

Susan walked towards the back door.

"Susan!" she heard Alex call out. "Help me!"

Susan ran out the door and around the house. Alex lay on the ground with the ladder beside him. She could tell by the look on his face that he was in pain.

"Alex! Are you okay?" she cried. "Oh, no you aren't! Look at that leg!" She turned toward the house. "Sarah! Call Doc Stanton!"

Alex's leg was most definitely broken. It lay twisted beneath him.

"Just try to lay back, honey. The doctor is coming," she told him.

He winced in pain. "I knew that ladder was on its last leg," he told her.

"Well, now so are you," she told him.

He smiled weakly at her.

The doctor came quickly. After one look at Alex, he said, "Well you won't be doing any climbing for a while, friend."

They loaded Alex up into the van, and Susan drove him to the hospital.

"How are we going to manage the inn while I've got this bum leg?" Alex asked Susan.

"You don't worry about that," she said. "We will handle things while that leg heals."

◊◊◊

When Jodi got home that afternoon and learned what had happened to Dad, she ran into his room to see him. She found Dad lying in bed with Jesse drawing an airplane on his cast.

"Dad! Are you okay? I'm so sorry this happened to you." She gave him a big hug.

"It doesn't really hurt much," he said. "It's just this heavy cast that is a bummer."

"We'll do everything we can to help out, Dad. You just get that leg well. Right, Jesse?"

"Right, sis," said Jesse.

Jodi was very upset about her Dad. She went into the kitchen to talk with Mom.

"Mom, I know it's going to take a long time for Dad to be back on his feet," said Jodi. "I've been thinking about something that might help."

"You have? What is it?" Mom asked.

"You know Dave wanted to come here for a visit, but he said he needed a job to help pay his way. Do you think we could pay Dave to help out around the Sea Bird? I mean, at least while Dad is on the mend? He might even find something in town to do, too. What do you think?"

"That's not a bad idea," said Mom. "Let me talk to your dad about it. I'll let you know what we decide. Okay?"

"Great, Mom," Jodi said.

◊◊◊

Later that day, Mom told Jodi that she'd discussed the idea with Dad, and she could call Dave and see if he was interested in their idea.

When Dave answered the phone, Jodi felt that tingle go up her spine. It was the feeling she got every time she talked to him.

Dave was sorry to hear about Mr. Bennett's accident. He talked with his parents about the job, and they had no objections.

"I'll be there tomorrow afternoon, if that's okay," he told her.

"Oh, Dave, I can't wait to see you again," said Jodi.

"I'll be there before you know it," he told her. "Bye-bye, sweetie."

"Bye, Dave. I love you."

"Love you, too."

When Dave arrived the next day, he couldn't believe how beautiful it was at the inn.

"If I lived here, I would never want to leave," he said.

He gave Jodi a big hug, which let her know how much he had missed her.

"Savannah is beautiful, but this is so different," he told her.

"I hope you brought your camera with you," she said.

"It goes wherever I go," he told her. "Let's go check with your dad and see what jobs he has lined up for me."

"Well, let's get your suitcase in the house first," she laughed.

He gave her a quick kiss, and they walked up the steps and onto the front porch. Mom, Sarah and Jesse all came out to greet Dave. Jodi took him out on the back porch where Dad was sitting.

"Hello, Dave," said Dad.

"Hi, Mr. Bennet," said Dave. "I'm ready to start right away."

"That's good. First of all, let's welcome the new guests from Alabama. They should be here any time now. He's a football coach."

Harlon and Grace Fortner arrived about three o'clock. Dave greeted them, Susan signed them in, and Dave took their bags up to their room.

"I think he's an old hand at this," said Dad.

"He loves people, Dad. It just comes easily to him," said Jodi.

"Well, I think he will be a good hand to have around." He winked at Jodi. "I don't imagine you would object to that, would ya?" he laughed.

"Dad!" Jodi said as she blushed.

◊◊◊

Over the next few days, Dave began to learn how the routine went at the Sea Bird.

"I could get used to this," he said as Jodi walked by.

"Dad is so grateful for how much you have helped out, Dave," said Jodi. "I don't know how we would have made it without you. Doc Stanton says that Dad won't be back walking without crutches for another month at least. Mandy's mom said she could use some help at the Sand Dollar whenever you aren't busy here."

They looked at each other and smiled, then both went back to their chores.

One afternoon, when both Dave and Jodi were free for a while, she suggested that they go for a walk on the beach.

"Bring your camera, too. I want to take you to a very special place."

"Awesome! But any place where you are is special," he said as he winked at her.

Dave ran up to his room, grabbed his camera, and together, they walked hand in hand to the beach. and down to the lower reef. The tide was out, so they walked out onto the reef to look down into the water.

"I've never seen anything quite like this, Jodi," said Dave. "It's beautiful."

"Look at the colors, Dave. Isn't it awesome?"

He got out his camera and began taking pictures. Excitement shone on his face.

Jodi grinned. "I knew you would love this. That's why I wanted you to come here."

"You do know me well, don't you Jodi?" he said as he pulled her close.

"Well, I like to think I do," she said with a smile.

Dave pulled her into his arms and kissed her. "I love you, Jodi. I don't ever want to be away from you again."

"I feel the same way, Dave. I think we are real soul mates. We think alike. We like the same things."

"Thank you for bringing me here. I want to come back and take more pictures when the light is different. I can't get enough of this."

"I know. I've painted this place before. A girl I went to school with bought the painting because she recognized the place. She said it was where she went when her spirits were down.

"I can understand that," Dave said. "It makes me feel good, too."

Chapter 30

"Jesse, can you bring me that tablet and a pencil from my desk?" said Dad.

"Sure, Dad," Jesse called back.

"I want to plan out the front garden for the fall," he told Jesse.

"Can I help you, Dad?" he asked.

"Sure thing, buddy. You can help me get to the front porch so I can see the garden."

Jesse carried out the tablet and pencil for his dad and held the door open until he got to his chair.

"Thanks, buddy," said Dad. "Doors can be a little tricky with crutches."

With their heads together, they talked about the flower beds and what they wanted to plant this fall. Susan brought out some milk and cookies that Sarah had just finished baking.

"Tell Sarah these are just what we needed for planning flowers," Alex told her.

"She'll be glad to hear that," she said as she went back inside.

Dave came up on the porch and took a look at Alex's list and drawings.

"Looks like you have a big job ahead of you," he said. "I can get that bed dug up for you this afternoon if you want. Jesse can give me a hand with the digging. Right, kiddo?"

"Sure thing Dave! I like digging."

"When you get your list completed, Jesse and I can go into Windy Point to get the supplies for the garden."

"You can take the van and pick up the plants while you are there too," Alex told him.

◊◊◊

"I don't know what we would have done without Dave's help," Alex told Sarah later that afternoon. "He thinks of what needs to be done before I even say anything to him."

"I think *our* daughter has good taste in men, don't you?" said Sarah.

"Yes, she does. She sure does."

She winked at him as she went back to her work.

◊◊◊

Jodi had been out on the beach painting again. Today was a little overcast, so the colors would be completely different from the last painting she'd done here. That was what was so amazing about painting. The results always varied depending on factors like the weather and the intensity of the light. The water, of course, was always changing colors because of its movement. She had taken several pictures of this spot before beginning her work. This time, her focus was on the sky.

I want to get this purple and gray just above the water, she thought, *then fade upwards into the lighter parts of the clouds.*

She could see it already forming on the canvas. As she painted, a sliver of light broke through behind the clouds and outlined the edges. Again, she snapped a picture.

"I don't want to lose this one," she told herself.

The proverbial silver lining, she thought.

When it was too dim for her to paint anymore, she gathered up her easel and supplies and headed back to the inn. As she approached the house, she could see some activity out in the front yard. Dave and Jesse were busily digging up the flower bed.

"I see you two have been busy," she told them.

"I'm cracking the whip every time they slow down," said Dad from the porch.

She laughed as she gave Dave a quick kiss on the check.

"Ooh la la!" teased Jesse.

"You just wish you had a girl as pretty," Dave teased back.

"That's okay. I have the best big sister ever," Jesse said proudly.

"Aw, thanks, little bro," she answered as she gave him a hug.

When she passed her dad on the porch, he whispered, "He's a keeper, honey."

"I know, Dad," she said and hugged his neck.

Mr. and Mrs. Fortner came out onto the porch with glasses of iced tea, looking for empty rockers. Alex invited them to sit and enjoy the view before dinner.

"I just love this big, old porch," said Grace. "It reminds me of Granddaddy's farm back home in Alabama."

"Except for the ocean, dear. There was no ocean view there," said Harlon.

"Of course not, Harlon. There wouldn't be an ocean in the middle of a tobacco field," she laughed.

"I hear you are a football coach, Mr. Fortner," said Dave.

"Yes, I am, son. I coached at a high school in Alabama. Do you play?"

"I played in high school. The college I went to didn't have sports." He turned to Jesse and called, "Jesse, go get your football! Maybe the coach can give you some pointers."

Jesse ran up to his room to retrieve the ball, and the boys passed it back and forth for a while. Coach Fortner commented on how to hold the ball properly and how to tuck it in when running. Just about the time they were beginning to tire out, Sarah called to tell them that dinner was ready. One by one, they all went inside to wash up and join each other at the table. Jesse held the door for Alex as he hobbled inside.

"I won't be running for any touchdowns for a while," he told Jesse.

"That's okay, Dad. I don't mind helping you."

The conversation that night consisted of chrysanthemums, touchdown passes, and colors in a cloudy sky.

"I don't think we ever lack for a good subject to talk about here," said Susan, smiling.

"Such a lovely meal and good company to dine with," said Grace Fortner.

"Yes, it was. My compliments to the chef," said Harlon.

Sarah walked in to take her bows. "Wait until you taste my Key lime pie!" she chuckled as she refilled the coffee cups.

Chapter 31

Mr. Maxwell called to ask about more paintings for his gallery. By now, Jodi had six completed and was working on a seventh.

"I should have this one finished by tomorrow," she told him.

"I have a buyer here who loves your work and has been asking if there are more," said Mr. Maxwell.

"I will try to bring these in on Saturday."

"Wonderful. He won't be leaving Atlanta until next Wednesday."

Jodi talked with Dave about the trip, and he said he would be glad to drive her to the Artist's Eye. Fortunately, they wouldn't be busy at the inn this weekend.

"Why don't you bring some of your work too, Dave? I think Mr. Maxwell would love to see it."

"I'll see what I can put together before then," he told her.

On Friday, the two of them loaded up the van with her work.

"I can't wait for Mr. Maxwell to see the photographs you have taken, Dave," said Jodi. "I'm sure he will be as impressed with them as I am."

It was good to be able to spend some time alone. Jodi and Dave hadn't been able to do much of that at the inn. Dave took her hand in his while he drove. She just looked at him and smiled happily. She was so happy to have met this man. He looked at her and winked. What was it Abbey had called them? "Two peas in a pod."

◊◊◊

Peter Maxwell invited them into his office.

"Jodi, Dave, so good to see you both again," he said.

"You too, Mr. Maxwell," said Jodi. "I hope you will be pleased with the work I brought for you."

"Oh Jodi, I don't ever worry about liking your work!"

She smiled and blushed a little.

"Let's see what you have for me this time."

The paintings were laid out on his table for his approval.

"Beautiful!" he said. "They just keep getting better and better! I'm amazed at this one with the beach and the cloudy sky. Just look how the sun is coming through the edges of the cloud. Jodi, Jodi . . . just lovely."

"Mr. Maxwell, do you remember that Dave is a photographer?" she asked.

"Why, yes, I do seem to remember that you were taking classes in photography, Dave. Do you have some of your work with you?"

"I did bring a few samples with me, at Jodi's insistence," said Dave.

"Well, let's see them."

Dave opened up his case and showed his work.

"Well, well," said Mr. Maxwell. "I like what I see so far. It seems you specialize in black and white. Is that right?"

"I think the photographs are more dramatic that way," said Dave.

"I agree with you wholeheartedly. They make more of a statement. I like these underwater shots of the reef. I would like to see more, Dave. Can you make up a portfolio for me?"

"Sure, I can do that," Dave said, beaming.

"The two of you are very talented," said Mr. Maxwell.

"I think we both have the same love for it," said Jodi.

"It shows in your work," he told them. "Dave, here is my card. Give me a call when you have something put together for me."

"I certainly will, Mr. Maxwell. Thank you so much."

As they walked back to the car, Jodi looked at Dave proudly.

"I knew he would like your work. Just think, our work could be hanging in the same gallery."

"I like that idea, don't you?" he said with a grin. "Side by side," he added as he kissed her.

Arm in arm, they walked down the street and back to the car.

◊◊◊

After Jodi and Dave left the gallery, Mr. Maxwell received a phone call.

"Peter Maxwell here . . . Yes, Miss Bennett just left. I have seven more for you . . . Very good. I will see you in the morning."

He hung up the phone and settled back into his chair, a very pleased look on his face.

Chapter 32

Back at the Sea Bird, things were going fairly normally. There were still a few guests coming and going, but the busy season was drawing to an end. Doc Stanton had told Alex that if things continued as they were, he would be able to remove the cast in another week or two. Alex was glad to hear that. He was not the type to sit and watch other people working and couldn't wait to get back to his chores around the inn. Susan spoke often about how helpful Dave was around the place.

"He's taken on a lot in a short time, hasn't he?" said Alex.

"Yesterday, he even booked some new guests for next week," said Susan. "I was sure that we wouldn't have many staying here by this time of the season."

"He knows how to talk to people and how to make them want to stay," said Alex. "I think he has a natural talent for running an inn like this. Jodi said he was good with people, didn't she?"

"He's sure been good for Jodi, I know that," Susan replied.

When Dave came in, he asked Alex if there was anything he needed for him to do.

"Son, I think we are caught up for the moment, don't you?" said Alex.

"I just wanted to be sure I wasn't overlooking anything," Dave answered.

"The garden's looking nice," said Susan. "You and Jesse did a fine job out there. Those flowers really add a lot of color to the place."

Jesse came in just in time to overhear the conversation. "Sparky even helped to dig some of the holes for the flowers," he said.

"Just so he doesn't dig them back up," said Dad.

"I'll watch to see that he doesn't."

"Mr. Bennett, would it be ok if I took Jodi out for dinner tonight?" Dave asked.

"I don't see why not," said Alex. "Do you, Susan?"

"That's fine, Dave," she replied.

◊◊◊

Jodi was in town visiting with Mandy at the Sand Dollar. Together, they talked about how they had spent their summer.

"I wish I could do something exciting. I never get to go anywhere," said Mandy.

"Maybe the next time I take paintings to Atlanta, you can go too," said Jodi.

"That would be fun. I've never been to Atlanta."

"It's really an exciting place," said Jodi. "It's so busy and there are tons of lights and things to do and see. The Artist's Eye is a great place to see, Mandy. I can't wait for you to see my paintings hanging there. Now Dave's work might be there too! Isn't that great?"

"He's really a special guy, Jodi. I'm so glad you two met. He's perfect for you."

"Yeah, he is pretty special, isn't he?" Jodi replied with a dreamy look in her eyes. "Well, I guess I had better be going. Mom needs me to help out with desserts this afternoon."

"I know how that is," Mandy said. "I still have to sweep up the dining room."

Jodi got her bike and waved goodbye as she headed back down the road towards home.

Dave was standing on the front porch when she pedaled into the driveway.

"Well, hi there, pretty girl," he called to her.

"Hey, Dave, are you waiting for me?"

"Yeah. I wanted to know if you would like to go to dinner with me tonight. Your mom and dad said it would be okay."

"Sure, I would. I have to help Mom with some desserts this afternoon. After that, I am free."

"Great! How about seven?"

"I'll be ready. You *know* where I live," she giggled.

This would be one of the first real dates they'd had since Dave had come to Windy Point.

A little later, Mom was stirring up the cake batter while Jodi made cake frosting. Sarah had taken the day off.

"We'll make the chocolate cake first, then the cherry pie. Okay?" said Mom.

Jodi was staring out the window.

"Jodi, did you hear me?"

"Oh!" said Jodi. "Sorry, Mom, I guess I was daydreaming a bit."

"What's on your mind, honey? Something I can help you with?"

"No, not really. I was just thinking about Dave, as usual." She laughed.

"Nothing wrong with that, dear. He's a really sweet guy. You know your Dad and I like him."

"I just hate the thought of him ever leaving here," Jodi said.

"Well, he doesn't *have* to leave Jodi."

"When Dad's leg is healed, we won't need him anymore, will we?"

"We've gotten used to having him here. He's such a big help to us all. I think we could keep him on even after Dad's back on his feet. Maybe he could find some photography work here to do, too."

"I know he loves it here, Mom. Maybe he would want to stay."

"I guess that would be up to Dave, don't you think?"

"I guess so Mom."

◊◊◊

At seven o'clock, Dave knocked on Jodi's bedroom door.

"I have a date with the prettiest girl in town. Is she ready?" he called through the door.

"Let me check," said Jodi. "Yes, she says she will be out in a minute," she laughed.

When she opened the door, Dave's face lit up. She was wearing her long dark, hair down and loose, and it looked lovely over her shoulders.

"Looking into your eyes, I get the strangest tingle down my spine," said Dave.

Jodi smiled. "I thought I was the only one who felt that way."

"You look very nice, Jodi. I haven't seen you in a dress very often."

"I thought I might like to try something different tonight."

"It certainly works for me," he said.

After telling her parents goodnight, they left for town in Dave's car.

"Where are we going?" she asked.

"Someplace special for my special girl," he said and winked.

They drove almost into town, and Dave pulled over to a place where the road ran close to the ocean. He parked the car, and they got out. He opened the trunk of the car. Inside, there was a large picnic hamper, two folding chairs, and a small folding table.

"What is all of this?" asked Jodi.

"A special dinner for my special girl," he told her.

Together, they carried everything down to the beach. Dave set up the table and chairs while Jodi spread the tablecloth over the little table. Inside the hamper, she found a set of candle holders and candles and a little bouquet of flowers.

"How sweet, Dave!"

They began setting the table and laying out all the food.

"Sarah fixed all of this for us yesterday," said Dave. "It looks like she did a great job. She even put in a bottle of non-alcoholic wine for us." He grinned as he filled two glasses for them.

"Leave it to Sarah to think of everything," said Jodi.

"That's for sure," he said.

The sun was just going down over the water as they lit the candles and drank the wine. Dave served the food, and as they ate, they gazed dreamily into each other's eyes.

"This is such a romantic thing for you to do, Dave," said Jodi.

As the sun sunk slowly below the water's horizon, he took her hand.

"Jodi, you are all I think about morning, noon, and night," he said. "When you left Atlanta and I had to go back to Savannah, I didn't think I would be able to be away from you. Now that we are together again, I want to keep it that way. I don't ever want to leave you again. I love you, Jodi. Will you marry me, Jodi? I want you to be my wife."

"Oh, Dave!" Jodi gasped. "Oh my goodness, of course I will marry you! I love you, Dave. I think I fell in love with you the day I first met you."

Big tears rolled down her checks.

"Don't cry, Jodi. Did I upset you? I didn't mean to—"

"No, no, you didn't, Dave. These are happy tears!" she said as she hugged his neck.

He reached into his jacket pocket and pulled out a tiny box. He opened it and took out a gold ring with a little diamond set in it.

"I know it's not a big, impressive stone, but it's all I can do right now," he said as he slipped it on her finger.

"Sweetheart, it's beautiful! It's all I need, and this has been better than some exclusive restaurant."

Jodi kissed him. This time, she felt that tingle run down her back again. She wondered if Dave was feeling the same tingle.

"We can get married when I have a real job so that I can support us both."

They talked about their future together while they sat out under the stars. What a beautiful night this was for both of them.

Chapter 33

"Dave, can I speak with you for a moment?" said Alex.

"Sure Mr. Bennett, what's up?"

Alex was in a rocker out front on the porch. "Sit down here and talk with me."

Dave pulled another rocker over close to Alex's chair and got comfortable.

"From what I hear," said Alex, "you and my daughter have gotten very serious about each other. Is that right?"

"Yes, it is, Mr. Bennett. I really love Jodi, and I want to spend my life with her," said Dave.

"Well, you know Susan and I really think a lot of you, Dave. We never could have done without you all these weeks. Now, if you and Jodi are going to get married, then you will need a full-time job in order to support the two of you."

"I know that, Mr. Bennett. I told Jodi that we might have to wait."

"Susan and I have been thinking. You know, I will get my cast off in a week or two, but I think I might still need some help here. You have shown me some things that I think would be good improvements at the inn, and I'd like you here to help me follow through with them. You have a good head on your shoulders, and you're great with people. We both think you would be a real asset here at the Sea Bird. What would you think if I offered you a sort of partnership with Susan and I here at the inn?"

"Are you serious? Of course, I would like that!" said Dave. "I love it here. I love the house. I love working with the guests. And, of course, I already love your family."

"Well, you and Jodi just set a date, and then you and I will have to sit down and do some figuring on paper to do just that."

Dave could hardly contain his excitement. He couldn't wait to tell Jodi the news.

◊◊◊

"Well, what did he say?" asked Susan.

"The poor boy almost bowled me over accepting!" laughed Alex.

"That's wonderful. Jodi will be thrilled when she hears this. He will make a great son-in-law, don't you think, Alex?"

"He sure will. I already love the guy," said Alex.

◊◊◊

After Dave's talk with Alex, all Jodi and Dave could think about was getting married.

"I don't want a big wedding," said Jodi. "I want to be married on the beach just before sunset. Can you imagine the colors in the sky at that time! It would be awesome. I can have a long, delicate white dress that will just float in the beach air."

She could almost see the picture on canvas.

"You would look beautiful like that," said Dave, "with your long hair down on your shoulders just like that special night on the beach."

"This is like a dream answered," she said as she looked deep into his big, dark eyes.

"It's been my dream, too," he told her.

They decided that if it was a beach wedding they wanted, it would have to be soon. The weather would be turning colder before long. Susan and Jodi talked about their plans.

"I think mid-September would be about right," said Mom. "What do you think, Jodi?"

"That doesn't give us much time," said Jodi. "Would we be able to get everything ready?"

"Well, you won't have to worry about where you will have it. Of course, it can be right here at the Sea Bird. Sarah and I can do all the food. You can have the ceremony right out there on the beach if you like."

"Wow, Mom, sounds like you have already been giving this some thought."

"I've always dreamed of your wedding day, Jodi. Now, it's just coming true."

"It sounds perfect. Just what I want."

"We'll have to go look for your dress soon," said Mom.

Jodi could already see this bridal scene on her canvas. She saw the colors in the sky while she and Dave repeated their vows to each other. She could see her dress rippling in the breezes from the ocean. Her dream was coming true right before her eyes.

"Dave, tell me how you see our wedding," Jodi said when the two of them were alone. "Is there anything special you would like to have?"

"Just you," he said. "That's all I need." He smiled.

"Isn't there anything you can think of?"

"Let me think . . . The decorations . . . I want everything decorated with a beach theme. Is that okay with you?"

"Perfect!" she said. "I'll talk with Mom and Sarah. I'm sure we can do that."

◊◊◊

The following Saturday, Susan and Jodi had plans to go to Athens to look for Jodi's wedding gown. They left early that morning and arrived just after ten. The bridal shop had lots of gowns to look at, and they began their search for the perfect dress.

"It's a beach wedding, so I want something long and flowing," Jodi told the saleswoman.

"I think I have a few that might be just right for you."

After collecting a few dresses, the saleswoman returned to the dressing room.

"That one looks too heavy for the beach," said Mom.

"I like this one with the delicate layers of lace on the skirt," said Jodi.

"Why don't you try that one on?" said Mom.

The dress fit her perfectly. It was long and flowing and showed her shape beautifully. Her long, dark hair looked beautiful on her shoulders.

"It's just what you described," said Mom.

"Yes, it is. I love this one!"

"What about adding this beaded belt to it?" suggested the saleswoman.

"Oh yes!" said Mom. "That really is beautiful, Jodi!"

"And now, shall we try a veil?"

"Perfect!" said Jodi.

When she stood in front of the mirror after adding the veil, big tears rolled down her checks.

"Oh, Mom!" she said. "Is this real?"

"Very much so, Jodi! I think we have found the right one. Don't you?"

"I do, I do," Jodi laughed as she wiped the tears. "I just had a tingle go up my spine."

"Well then, that says it all," said the saleswoman.

The ride home from Athens with the new gown was thrilling for the two of them.

"I saw the perfect dress for me at a shop in Windy Point," said Mom. "It's a delicate blue chiffon. Would that be all right?"

"That color would look awesome on you, Mom," said Jodi. "I'll have to go look for a ring for Dave sometime next week."

"I have Grandmother Bennett's earrings and necklace for you to wear. That can be your something old."

"Oh Mom! That set is gorgeous!"

"Now we have to think of something borrowed," said Mom. "What about your flowers?"

"You know, I've been thinking about that. Would it be strange to have chrysanthemums? They make me think of Dave, since he planted ours at the inn."

"I don't see why not. White mums would be beautiful, and you can mix in some other colors with them."

Chapter 34

The Wedding

After a few weeks of planning, the wedding day finally arrived. The weather was perfect for a wedding on the beach. Wedding guests were already arriving at the Sea Bird, and excitement was in the air.

Dave's parents, Big Dave and Patricia Langley, arrived the day before and were getting settled in.

"I'm in love with your home, Susan," said Patricia. "Big Dave and I would love to have a place like this. No wonder Dave wants to stay here."

"Thank you, Patricia. We have certainly loved having Dave here with us," said Susan.

"So much so, we decided to keep him," laughed Alex.

"He's getting a terrific little girl out of the deal," said Big Dave.

"I'll have to agree with you there," said Alex.

"They both are good children," said Sarah. "I would be proud to have either one of them as my own. By the way, Susan, may I see you for a minute?"

The two of them walked into the kitchen.

"What is it, Sarah?" asked Susan.

"I have something I want Jodi to wear in her wedding," said Sarah. "It can be the something borrowed. It belonged to my Grandmother."

She reached into her apron pocket and took out a little box. Inside was a tiny ring with a pearl set in it.

"Since I never had children, I don't have a daughter to pass it on to," said Sarah. "I would like her to wear it if she wants to."

"Oh, how sweet of you Sarah! I'm sure Jodi would love to wear it. It's so delicate, and it goes so well with the beach theme she has."

Susan gave Sarah a big hug.

"It's hard to believe she is so grown up already," said Sarah. "I feel like she is my daughter, too."

"Alex and I can certainly share her with you, Sarah," said Susan.

"I've always thought of her as my own daughter, Susan," said Sarah.

◊◊◊

It was time for the ceremony to begin. Dave stood nervously at the end of a long, green carpet they had laid out on the beach. It was lined with bouquets made from sea wheat and orange and yellow chrysanthemums. There were seashells scattered all along the edges of the carpet. At the end, where the preacher stood, there were two large bouquets of yellow and orange chrysanthemums with palm leaves.

As the music started, the groomsmen escorted the three bridesmaids down the aisle. They wore peach-colored dresses that matched the flowers Jodi had chosen. Mandy was her maid of honor. Mr. Langley was Dave's Best Man.

Dave walked down the aisle and came to a stop at the end to wait for his bride. As the wedding march began, Alex walked arm in arm down the aisle with Jodi. She was radiant in her beautiful, lacy gown. Susan looked so proud to be her mother. Jesse sat with his mother and waited for Jodi. Alex was a little tearful as he stopped to hand her off to Dave.

Dave took one long look at Jodi and felt that tingle again. Jodi felt it too. As the preacher led them through their vows and the exchanging of rings, they looked lovingly at each other as they repeated them.

"I now pronounce you man and wife," said the preacher.

Dave lifted Jodi's veil and took her in his arms.

"I love you, Mrs. Langley," he told her.

"I love you too, Mr. Langley," she replied.

They gave each other a long, sweet kiss. The audience applauded. They smiled at each other and walked back down the aisle.

◊◊◊

Back at the Sea Bird, everyone was gathering for the reception. Jodi and Dave posed for pictures before cutting the beautiful wedding cake Sarah and Susan had made for them. It was decorated perfectly with tiny seashells and starfish. When it came time to toss the bridal bouquet, it was Mandy who caught it.

"You are next!" shouted Jodi.

Mandy blushed and laughed, "Maybe someday, my prince will come."

That night, Dave and Jodi had reservations at a hotel in a neighboring town for their honeymoon.

"Someday, we will have a real honeymoon, my love," he told her.

"This is all I need," said Jodi. "I just want to spend it with you."

She had never been happier. Tonight, that tingle they kept feeling would be joined between them.

"I love you, Jodi," Dave said as they fell asleep.

"I love you too, Dave."

Chapter 35

After the honeymoon was over, Jodi and Dave returned to the inn. Jodi's bedroom had been decorated for the new bride and groom. She still had room for her paintings, and now, there was a place for Dave's things too. Along with some of Jodi's paintings on the wall, there were Dave's photographs. They each admired the other's work and were glad to share the space.

Every morning when they woke up next to each other, in bed they said to each other, "Is this real?"

"I can't believe I am so lucky to have you for my wife," he told her.

"I'm so glad we found each other," she told him.

"And we get to do this every day!" he laughed at her.

"I wouldn't have it any other way," she said with a grin.

"I have an announcement to make," said Dad at breakfast. "Doc Stanton wants me to come in today to have the cast removed!"

"Hooray!" said Jesse.

"Hooray is right, son! No more crutches!" replied Dad.

"I don't want you to overdo it, though," said Susan.

"I know. Doc Stanton already warned me about that, honey."

"Remember, you still have help whenever you need it, Mr. Bennett," said Dave.

"That's good to know, Dave. But do you know what? I think it's time you called me Alex."

"Well, okay, Alex, if you want me to," said Dave.

"So, Dad, are you going to start calling Jodi Mrs. Langley? said Jesse.

"I wouldn't go that far, son," Alex laughed and tousled Jesse's hair. "She'll always be my little girl."

◊◊◊

Sarah was just putting the finishing touches on lunch when Alex got back from the doctor.

"Well, it sure is good to see you without those cumbersome crutches, Alex," she told him.

"It sure is, Sarah," he said. "I'm still not very stable yet. I can see I will have to take it slow for a while. Susan was right."

Dave was coming in the back door as Alex arrived.

"I repaired that old ladder," he said. "Now I can finish up those shingles you've been working on."

"*Be careful!*" everyone said at once.

Sparky barked.

"Sparky says so, too," said Jesse.

They all laughed, but they knew they were serious about this.

"I see you can never be too careful," Alex assured them. "Dave, I wanted to talk with you about the firepit you suggested. I think that would be a great thing to have when the weather gets colder."

"Yeah, I think the guests would enjoy sitting around it, drinking some hot chocolate or apple cider," said Dave.

"This new son-in-law of mine has some great ideas, doesn't he, Susan?" said Alex as he patted Dave on the back.

"That's my new husband!" Jodi said, beaming.

"Dave, I think they are going to keep you," said Jesse.

They all laughed at this.

"What do you say we go figure out how many bricks we will need for that new firepit?" said Alex.

"Ready when you are, Alex," said Dave.

After the two had left, Jodi turned to Susan and said, "Mom, I am so glad that Dad and Dave get along so well."

"Isn't it wonderful, Jodi?" she said. "We both love Dave. We couldn't ask for a better son-in-law or a better husband for you."

"Thanks, Mom. I know how special he is."

◊◊◊

Dave, Dad, and Jesse drove into town to buy the needed materials for the firepit. By that afternoon, it was almost finished.

"Looks good, Dave," said Alex.

"I'll see about getting some wood stocked up to burn in it," said Dave.

"Good idea."

"I've been thinking about building some benches around it. Nothing too fancy. Maybe some stationary benches anchored into the ground. What do you think, Alex?"

"I like that idea. Something the weather won't bother."

"I'll check on that tomorrow."

New guests arrived that afternoon from Cleveland: Tom and Hannah Waverly. Tom was a retired pilot who had served in the Army for over forty years. Hannah had also been in the Army as a flight nurse, and Tom was returning to Georgia for a reunion with some of his fellow war buddies.

"What a beautiful place!" said Hannah as they came up the front steps.

Dave welcomed them and brought their luggage inside. "Welcome to the Sea Bird," he told them.

Susan came in to get acquainted. "How was your trip?" she asked.

"My husband flew us down from Cleveland," said Hannah. "We landed in Atlanta and then drove here. It was a wonderful drive."

"So, you are a pilot then?" said Susan.

"Retired Army pilot. Over forty years flying planes," said Tom.

"Wow!" said Jesse, popping his head out from around the corner. "That's awesome, Mr. Waverly. I love airplanes! I make models of them."

"You do?" said Tom. "My grandson does, too. We'll just have to have a look at yours."

Dave was out in the backyard working on the benches he and Alex had talked about. He was just finishing up the last one when Jesse ran up with Sparky.

"What do you think about trying out this firepit tonight?" said Dave. "We could roast marshmallows in the fire."

"Awesome, Dave! I'll go ask Mom if we have any."

"We need some long sticks to roast them on," Dave told him.

"We used to use coat hangers for that," said Jesse. "I'll see if we have any extras around."

"How about some hot chocolate to go with that?" said Jodi as she walked over to the pit.

"Sounds like a plan to me, sweetie," Dave commented. He kissed Jodi on the tip of her nose, then added, "But you won't need any."

"Why not?"

"Because you are already sweet enough," he laughed. He took her into his arms and gave her a long kiss. "See, I taste chocolate already."

"Silly," she said and smiled at him.

"And I *love* chocolate," he said.

"And I *love* you," she answered.

◊◊◊

After dinner that night, Dave got the firepit started, and the Sea Bird guests came out to enjoy it.

"Awesome, Dave!" said Jesse. "Mom gave me some marshmallows."

"Here are the coat hangers, son," said Dad. "I've already bent them into shape for you."

"Thanks, Dad," said Jesse.

The other guests found seats on the benches so they could enjoy the fire.

"Anyone want hot chocolate? I have some right here," said Sarah.

"That sounds like a good idea," said Mr. Waverly.

Sarah poured cups for Mr. Waverly and his wife. Sparky was running around, trying to catch the sparks floating around the fire.

"Little dog, if you catch one of those, you may have more energy than you already do," laughed Mrs. Waverly.

"This almost takes me back to camping days with my buddies," said Tom Waverly. "We used to sit around the campfire and tell each other stories."

"Can you tell us one, Mr. Waverly?" asked Jesse.

"Well, son, let me see if I can remember one. There was the time I was flying over Germany and we ran out of gas."

"Wow! What did you do?" asked Jesse.

"We prayed a lot. I can tell you that much. Then we looked for a farmer's field to land in. Just about the time the old engine started to sputter, we saw a break in the clouds. Wouldn't you just know, there was a little field just below us. We circled around and dropped altitude and let that old buggy just glide its way in. We managed to land with just one or two hard bumps. I can tell you, the Man Upstairs was with us that day!"

"It must be awesome to fly," said Jesse.

"It is, son, but you have to mind your Ps and Qs while you are doing it."

"Like remembering to fill the gas tank?" Jesse said.

"You got that right, buddy!" said Tom as he patted Jesse on the back.

Alex could tell that this firepit would get a lot of good use. He had Dave to thank for that.

Chapter 36

Late in the afternoon, Jodi received a telephone call from Jack Parker.

"Mr. Parker! It's such a surprise to hear from you," she said.

"Yes, it has been quite a while since we spoke, hasn't it?" said Jack.

"Yes, it has. How are you and Mrs. Parker doing?"

"It's been a long, hard ride, but we are making it. Listen, Jodi, the reason I called is I am hosting a showing for a young artist here next month. I would like for you to be here to see it. Do you think you can come? It will be on December fourteenth."

"I'll have to get back with you on that. Since you were here, I have gotten married, so I will have to discuss this with my husband."

"Well, congratulations Jodi! That's wonderful. Yes, call me back when you've had time to talk about it. I think this showing will be an enlightenment for you. You and your husband are more than welcome to stay here with Meredith and I while you are in New York. We have plenty of room. We can also make all the arrangements for your flight."

"That sounds very exciting, Mr. Parker. I will call you back as soon as I can to let you know."

"Thanks, Jodi. We'll be waiting to hear from you."

After she hung up the phone, she couldn't wait to tell Dave about the offer.

◊◊◊

Jack Parker called back later that day to talk with Alex and Susan.

"I talked to your daughter earlier today to invite her to an art showing up here in New York," Jack explained. "I didn't want to tell Jodi that the showing is *hers*. I've been buying her work in Atlanta from Peter Maxwell every chance I could. Peter never told her that I was her buyer. Please don't spoil my secret for her."

"Her mother and I have always known that she has great talent, but we didn't expect things to happen this quickly," said Alex.

"People here who have viewed Jodi's work are already expressing their enthusiasm," said Jack. "Jodi will do well here. I'm sure of that."

"Alex and I will encourage her to go to New York," said Susan. "We want the best for her."

"That's great," said Jack. "Have her call me."

"We will," said Alex.

◊◊◊

Dave was as excited about the offer as Jodi.

"Of course, you have to go, sweetie," he told her.

"He wants us both to come, Dave. We can stay with them while we are there. I really would love to see his gallery."

"Well then, it's all set," said Dave. "Call him back and tell him we will be there."

When they went down to tell Jodi's parents, Alex and Susan seemed surprised and delighted by the news.

"It will be like another little honeymoon for the two of you," said Susan.

"Don't worry about things here. We can hold down the fort while you guys are gone," Alex told them.

"Are you sure, Dad? You know your leg isn't really strong just yet," said Jodi.

"That's true, but my little buddy here can help out," he said as he put his arm around Jesse.

"We make a good team, don't we Dad?" said Jesse.

"We sure do, little buddy," Dad told him.

Sparky barked at this.

"Okay, Sparky," said Jesse. "You can be part of the team, too."

The next few days were very busy. Dave and Jodi were getting things ready for their trip to New York.

"I've never been that far from home before," Jodi told Dave.

"I haven't either, but we will be doing this together," he said.

"I think this will be a very special trip for us."

"If I'm with you, it will always be special."

Dave gave her a long kiss. The tingle was back again.

Chapter 37

The plane was coming to a stop on the tarmac, rolling closer to the terminal. Jodi could already see the outline of the city in the distance. Jack had told them he would meet them at the airport.

Dave and Jodi walked down the ramp into the unloading area.

"I wonder if Mr. Parker is here yet," she said.

"I think we should stay right here and wait for him," said Dave. "We can get our luggage after we find him."

"It's such a huge place. I sure wouldn't want to get lost here."

Jodi stared down the long aisles that went off in every direction. After they had waited for a few minutes longer, they heard an announcement over the PA system: "Miss Jodi Bennett and party . . . please meet your party in the waiting room on Aisle B."

Dave stepped to the desk and asked the way to Aisle B.

"Follow this corridor to 310, take a left, and Aisle B is on the right," said the clerk.

"Thank you very much," said Dave.

They walked down the corridor and soon found the waiting room. Jack Parker approached them as soon as they entered.

"Jodi, it's so good to see you again," said Mr. Parker. "You must be Dave, her new husband. I'm so happy for you both."

"Mr. Parker," said Jodi. "How nice to see you again."

"Let's go get your luggage and be off. Show me your ticket, and I will lead the way."

"This place is like a maze," said Dave.

"I'm here a lot," said Jack with a grin.

Soon, they were in Jack's car, heading for his apartment.

"Look at all this traffic!" said Jodi. "And I thought Atlanta was busy!"

"Meredith is excited to see you, Jodi," said Jack.

"It will be nice to see her again, too," she said.

When they got out of the elevator in Jack's building, Meredith was already at the door to welcome them.

"Come in, come in!" she said. "I'm so glad that you and your new husband could come. How wonderful, Jodi. Welcome, both of you."

"Thank you so much for letting us stay with you, Mrs. Parker," said Jodi.

"Nonsense, we have plenty of room here. There are just the three of us," she said as she gave Jack a wink.

Jodi was a little puzzled by this.

"Maybe we should share our little secret with Jodi and Dave," Jack suggested.

"Of course," she said. "I'll be back shortly."

"So, how was your flight up?" asked Jack.

"For two who don't do much flying, it was awesome," said Dave.

"As much as I fly, I am still amazed by it," Jack told them.

Meredith came in through the hallway carrying a small, pink bundle. She was smiling brightly.

"This is our little secret," she said. "We have a new daughter."

Jodi's eyes lit up, and she gasped, "A new baby? A little girl? How very wonderful for you! May I see her?"

Meredith peeled back the blanket to reveal the most beautiful little girl Jodi had ever seen. She had curly, blond hair and deep blue eyes.

"She's gorgeous!" said Jodi. "Her eyes look . . . They look . . ." She hesitated.

"They look just like Sammy's," said Jack.

"We named her Samantha," said Meredith. "We knew we could never replace our son, but Samantha has helped to fill the hole he left in our hearts. Why don't you take our guests into the den, Jack?"

Jack swung open the double doors to take them inside. The focal point was a fireplace directly across the room from the doors. A painting hung above the mantle.

At first, Jodi thought she was seeing things. She looked first at Meredith, then at Jack.

"It can't be . . ." she said. "You have . . . It's Sammy! You have Sammy's Painting! Of course, you do. It should belong to you."

She broke down in sobs as she sat down on the couch.

"When Mr. Maxwell told me he sold it," said Jodi between sobs, "I was almost heartbroken. I really didn't want to let it go. It had become so much a part of me. Sammy was such a part of our lives while he was with us."

"We know that, Jodi," said Meredith. "When Jack brought this painting home, I cried when I saw it. I knew who it was immediately, even before I saw your name on it. The little dog was so lifelike. It was like our son was back with us again."

"This painting helped us get through our grief, Jodi," said Jack. "*You* helped us heal with your painting. Do you see how much feeling you put in your work? It's important that you know how very powerful that is."

They spent the next two hours getting reacquainted with each other. Dave was so proud of Jodi and what her work meant to people.

"Tomorrow is the showing at the art gallery," said Jack. "We should be there by nine."

That night, they all went out to a nice restaurant for dinner.

"It might not measure up to Sarah's fine dining, but it comes close," said Jack.

"It's beautiful here. Thank you for bringing us," said Jodi.

Jack held up his glass to make a toast. The others did the same.

"To all young artists everywhere," he said. "May they do well with their art."

"Agreed!" said the others.

◊◊◊

The next morning, they were up early having a nice breakfast with the Parkers.

"I have something here I want you to sign for me, Jodi," said Jack. "It's an agreement to show your work for any future shows I might have."

"Isn't that a little premature?" she asked.

"Not really. You never know when one might come up," he said.

After breakfast, he suggested they ride with him to the gallery. Meredith would be coming later after the sitter came to care for the baby.

When they arrived at the gallery, Jodi was impressed with its size.

"My goodness, I had no idea it was this large!" she said.

"It takes a lot of room to hold all of this art," Jack said.

The parking area was already filling up. People were coming in quickly.

"Your gallery must be a very popular place," she said.

"They are drawn by this new artist we are showing," Jack explained.

They went inside through the large, glass double doors. Inside was a large foyer. A huge chandelier hung overhead. People were standing in small groups everywhere Jodi looked.

And then, she saw it. In the middle of the foyer was a large easel with a sign that read:

INTRODUCING OUR NEWEST YOUNG TALENT
MISS JODI BENNETT
WINDY POINT, GEORGIA

"What is this?" said Jodi.

She looked at Jack who stood there, looking a little sheepish. "This is *your* showing Jodi," he said. "You are our newest young talent. Do you see what interest you have stirred? You just don't know when a showing might take place." He grinned.

"Is that what I signed for this morning?" she asked, a little flabbergasted.

"I think it was, Jodi," laughed Dave.

Jack led them down the hall where Jodi's work was on display. She stood and looked at her work hanging in this fabulous building.

"Is this real? My work, here in New York City?"

"Have you forgotten what I told you, Jodi?" Jack asked. "I said, you never know where your work might end up."

Jack led the two of them around the gallery and introduced Jodi to several art enthusiasts.

"I'm surprised at how young you are, Miss Bennett," commented one patron. "I really envisioned a much older woman."

"That just leaves many more years for her to improve," laughed Jack.

"She's far ahead of most older artists," stated one older gentleman.

"I agree fully," said Jack.

"Thank you, gentlemen," Jodi said as she blushed a little.

"Do you hear what people are saying, Jodi?" said Dave excitedly. "I heard one woman comment on your use of colors, and another man said that your children's faces were—what did he say? 'Believable.' That's how he put it."

"Believable," said Jodi. "I like that, don't you?"

"Yes, I do Jodi. And they are . . . really believable."

"You can see that there is a real market for your work here," Jack told her.

"It looks as though I will have to keep busy supplying you and Mr. Maxwell with my work!" said Jodi.

"It would seem so, Jodi."

◊◊◊

Once they had gotten back to the apartment, Jodi decided to call her mom to tell her everything that had happened.

"We know," said Mom, trying to hold back a laugh.

"You *know*? How could you know?" she asked.

"Jack called us after he talked with you about it. He told us everything, Jodi. We were so happy for you, honey."

"Did they tell you they have a new baby girl?" Jodi asked.

"No, they didn't! I'm so glad to hear that."

"She's beautiful, Mom. She has deep blue eyes just like Sammy. Her name is Samantha. Isn't that sweet? And do you know that they have Sammy's Painting hanging over their fireplace? I was so heartbroken when Mr. Maxwell sold it. Now, it couldn't be in a better place."

"That's amazing, honey. I think I know how that must have made you feel."

"I feel like that painting had a purpose, and now it has been fulfilled," she said.

"Yes, Jodi, I think you are right. And you were the one who made it happen. You and Dave have a great time while you are there. I'll tell Dad and Jesse you called. I love you, honey."

"I love you all, Mom."

Chapter 38

Things seemed very slow back in Windy Point, but the newlyweds were glad to be back.

"I couldn't live in a town that big, could you, Dave?" said Jodi.

"It was fun to visit New York, but it's much too fast-paced for me," said Dave. "I do wish we'd had time to take some photos while we were there. Maybe someday we can go back and do that."

"That would be fun," she said. "I wonder what kind of paintings I could do there."

Jodi smiled. It was funny how they both saw New York as a source for their artwork.

After a few days had passed, there was a package in the mail for Jodi. Inside was a New York newspaper with an article about the Jack Parker Art Gallery. It showed pictures of Jack with Jodi and Dave standing next to some of her paintings. The caption read: *YOUNG ARTIST MAKES BIG IMPRESSION IN NYC.*

"Wow! Would you look at that!" said Jodi.

Her small, coastal town upbringing lends to her "believable" art . . . read the article. *Jack Parker describes her as "on her way to the top."*

"I can't believe it," she said as she laid the paper down.

"We've all told you how good you are," said Mom.

"I know, Mom, but seeing it in the newspaper is so different."

"That's my girl!" said Dad.

"That's my big sister!" said Jesse.

Jodi grinned and ruffled his hair. "Jesse, you are the best little brother I have."

"Thanks, sis," he said as he left the room.

A few minutes later, he came back.

"Jodi, I'm your *only* little brother, aren't I?" he said.

"That's why you are the best," she laughed.

"Aw, sis, you're silly," he said.

◊◊◊

Jodi was in their room hanging up her clothes when Dave came in.

"Hey, sweetie," he said. "How about taking a break for a while?"

"What do you have in mind?" Jodi asked.

"I thought maybe you and I could take our cameras back down to the lower reef."

She hung up a few more pieces and said, "Sure. Today would be a good day. The sun isn't too bright. The lighting should be good for it. I only have a few more things to put away. Then we can go."

"Great. I'll get my camera and meet you downstairs."

"Okay. Be there in a sec."

A few minutes later, they were heading down the beach carrying their cameras.

"I came down here about two weeks ago, but the colors weren't showing up like I wanted them to," said Dave.

"Yeah, things have to be just right to get that perfect shot," she said.

They stepped across a few rocks to a ridge that stood up out of the water. It was a fairly flat place where they could stand and get some photos of the coral formations underwater.

"The water is very clear when the wind dies down, isn't it?" Dave said.

"Yes, some of these little pools hardly move at all."

"Look at the little fish swimming around that urchin."

He snapped a few pictures, fascinated by the underwater scene.

"Do you ever go snorkeling?" he asked.

"No, not in a long time. Do you?"

"A long time ago with my dad, but not recently."

"When the weather gets warmer, we should try it."

"If we had underwater cameras, we could get some fabulous shots. What do you think?"

"Sounds great. We'll have to remember that, come next spring."

Jodi looked overhead and watched a seabird circling the reef. As she raised her camera to take a shot, her foot hit a wet spot on the rocks, and she lost her balance. Dave caught her just as she slid into the water.

"Jodi! I got you, sweetie!"

They landed, sitting in a small pool of water. It had happened so fast that Jodi hadn't had time to be afraid. They took one look at each other sitting in the water with their clothes all wet and both of them started to laugh.

"Watch that first step," she said. "It's a doozy . . . The cameras! Where are they?"

"Here is yours. I still have mine around my neck," said Dave.

"I sure hope we didn't ruin them with the water," she said.

"They should be all right. They just got splashed a little."

"Well, I guess this photo shoot is over," she said as she stood up, wringing the water out of her jeans.

"We should get back and change before we catch a cold," he told her.

"It is a little too cool for a swim, isn't it?" she said with a grin.

When they got back to the inn, Susan gave them a funny look as they tried to slip in the back way.

"What happened to you two?" she asked.

"Let's just say the water was a little rough," giggled Jodi.

Chapter 39

The Waverlys returned that afternoon from Tom's reunion with his old Army buddies.

"He saw so many of his dear old friends. I'm so glad you decided to come," said Hannah.

"So am I, Hannah," he said a little sadly. "I wouldn't have missed this for the world. So many of us old geezers are passing on. I had best see the ones of us that are left while I can."

"I know, Dear, I know," she said. "A lot of the wives came, too, so I had some good folks to talk to."

"Well, that is so nice for you both," said Susan. "Would you like a nice cup of coffee and some of Sarah's fresh-baked cherry pie?"

"Oh, now doesn't that sound delicious, Hannah?" said Tom. "Of course we will."

"If you would like, I can serve you out on the front porch," said Susan. "The air is still nice out there."

"That would be wonderful, Susan," said Hannah. "Thank you so much."

"Mr. Waverly, would you like to see my model airplanes?" said Jesse.

"Sure thing, little buddy," he told him.

Jesse sat down on the porch in front of them and lined up the models he had completed. There was the Kamikaze that he had built with Sammy, the biplane glider, and the newest one that he and Dave had just finished: the B57 Bomber.

"Now that's quite a collection you have there!" said Tom. "I flew a bomber like that one a few times."

"Man! Did you drop any bombs?" said Jesse.

"Only when we had to, son. You know, war isn't very much fun. I'm glad it is over."

"Jesse, Mr. Waverly lost a lot of his buddies in those wars," said Hannah.

"I'm sorry, Mr. Waverly. I didn't know that. I guess we should be proud of those soldiers who fought."

"Yes, son, very proud indeed," said Mr. Waverly.

"We put our flag up on Memorial Day and Veteran's Day," Jesse told them.

"That's a fine thing to do, son. That's so we won't ever forget those soldiers that we have lost."

"Every time I look at my planes, I will remember that, Mr. Waverly. I won't forget."

"Thank you, son."

He looked at Hannah with tears in his eyes, but she didn't say anything. She had been a wartime nurse. She knew.

Chapter 40

Dave had been scouting the area around Windy Point for subjects to photograph and spent hours taking shots whenever he could. Today was Wednesday, and he had decided to go to the local newspaper office with a portfolio of his pictures. He had been thinking about the possibility of getting some kind of job with the newspaper.

Ben Dawson, editor of *The Windy Point Gazette* sat at his desk eating lunch when Dave came in.

"Morning there, son. What can I do for you?" he said.

"Well, sir, I was wondering if I could do something for you."

"Such as?" Ben asked.

Dave continued, "I thought maybe you could use a good photographer here at the paper."

"And that would be you?" said Ben.

"Yes, sir, that would be me. I graduated from the Atlanta School of the Arts. I've done lots of freelancing since then, and I think I could be a real asset for your paper."

"How would I know what kind of work you do, son?"

"I have a folder of some of my work I can show you." He spread out a few of his pictures on the desk.

"These look pretty good, boy. How would you use them in my newspaper?"

"I thought maybe I could take pictures of some local businesses and sell ads for them."

"That might be a good idea. Like they say, 'A picture is worth 1,000 words.' Tell you what, I'll give you a whole page to sell. You got twenty-five three by three-inch ads running Saturday only. Twenty dollars each. You've gotta have them sold before next Wednesday. Think you can do it?"

"I'll do my best. When do I start?"

"Five minutes ago!" said Ben.

"Yes, sir!"

Dave turned on his heels and left. He had a lot of work to do before Wednesday.

◊◊◊

"I have a job, Jodi!"

"You do? Where?" she asked.

"At the newspaper office. I guess I am their new ad manager/photographer."

"What does it pay?" she asked.

He laughed. "I really don't know. Mr. Dawson barked at me so fast, I just knew I had to get to work! It's kind of a trial thing to see what I can do. I'm sure I can come up with something."

"You are very creative, Dave. I'm sure you will be just what he needs. I'm happy for you!"

"Thanks, sweetie. I am kind of excited about it!"

◊◊◊

"Oh, so you are that pretty, little Bennett girl's new husband."

"Yes, ma'am," Dave said to the owner of the Broad Street Bakery. "I'm Dave Langley. I'm the new ad man from the Gazette. I'd like to photograph your store and sell you an ad for the paper."

"Oh? That might be just what I need to perk up my business a little."

"Yes, ma'am, it just might," he offered. "The ad will run in Saturday's paper. Can I put you down for one?"

"I think I will let you try it."

"Thank you, Mrs. Burdock. The paper will bill you."

The next stop on Dave's list was The Sack & Go market run by Archie Fitzgerald.

"Mr. Fitzgerald, I'm Dave Langley," he introduced himself.

"I know you," said Archie. "You're the guy who married Alex Bennett's daughter aren't you?"

"Yes, sir, I am. I'm working at the Gazette as an ad manager, and I was wondering if I could sell you an ad in Saturday's paper. I can take a nice photo of your store. The bakery is doing one."

"Yeah, I guess you can do that. Have Ben send me the bill."

"Thank you, Mr. Fitzgerald, I'm sure you won't regret it."

"Aw, call me Fitz. Everyone else does."

"Ok Fitz. Sure thing."

Dave spent the next three days talking to shopkeepers about placing ads in the paper. He knew how to talk to people, and everyone figured that if the other shopkeepers ran one, so should they. He ended up with twenty-five out of thirty people taking him up on his offer. He spent the next day taking pictures at all of the shops that had taken out ads. After he had finished, he went back to the Sea Bird to develop his pictures. Alex had let Dave build a little developing room out back in the shed. It was just big enough to work with his chemicals and have a place to hang his photographs to dry. He'd even placed a red light just outside the door to let people know not to disturb him while he was in the developing stages.

As the pictures started to take shape in the solution, Dave could see that he had gotten some good shots.

"The people who placed the ads will be pleased with these," he told himself.

After the prints had dried, he took them inside to show Jodi.

"These are awesome, Dave!" she said. "I can identify every one of them. This is the bakery. Here is the grocery, the barbershop, the hardware store . . . These are great, Dave. I can see that the light was good for you."

"I guess I will take all these down to Mr. Dawson," said Dave. "I hope he will be satisfied with them."

"Good luck, sweetheart," Jodi told him.

"Bye, sweetie."

◊◊◊

"Son, I think you have a good start here," said Mr. Dawson. "We'll run these and see how much excitement they stir up. If they like these, then we will see about letting them run for the month. You'll get a percentage of every ad you sell. How about that?"

"That sounds good to me, Mr. Dawson," said Dave.

"I'll give you a call and let you know how they do."

"I'll be waiting to hear from you, sir."

◊◊◊

With Dave working on his photographs and ad sales, it gave Jodi some time for her painting. In the park, she found a little girl with worn clothes asleep on a bench. She was using a small backpack as a pillow. Next to her was a big, old dog who was standing guard over her. The look in the old dog's eyes told the story. Jodi began calling this painting *The Runaway*. She took out her camera and took the shot.

As she sketched the picture, she wondered where this little girl had come from. What had happened to make her leave home? Maybe she was just waiting for someone. Maybe she hadn't run away at all. But Jodi couldn't stop thinking about her. She worked with her colors and began painting the old dog's face. Those eyes were the key to this story.

The life in this painting, she thought.

She painted the little girl on the bench. She tried to show how tired she must be. Her blond hair lay in tangles around her face and shoulders. There were shadows on her face as the sunlight shined through the leaves overhead.

She stepped closer to the child as she lay sleeping. Jodi could see dried tears on her cheeks. Was she lost? The dog stepped forward as if to protect the girl. Jodi backed away, and he relaxed.

The painting was beginning to take shape now. The scene showed how protective the dog was of the child. She made sure to highlight the tear stains on her face. It became real, now.

Before Jodi went home, she stopped by Sheriff Thomas's office. She just could not shake the feeling that the little girl might be a missing child. She reported the little girl she had seen in the park. Sheriff Thomas said that he had not heard of anyone's child being missing, but he would look into it. Jodi was satisfied with that, so she went on home.

When she got back to the Sea Bird, she told Susan what had happened in the park.

"You did the right thing by telling the sheriff about it, Jodi," said Susan. "You just never know, these days."

"I know, Mom. It just bothered me. Ever since Sammy died, I just want to be so protective of children."

Late the next morning, there was a call for Jodi. It was Sheriff Thomas.

"I just wanted to call about the little girl you told me about yesterday," he said. "Charles Johnson out on Beachfront Drive called to tell me that his granddaughter had disappeared. When he said that she had a big, old dog with her, I knew it must be the same child. I went down to the park, and the little girl was still sitting there with this sad, old dog. I asked her where she lived, but all she could tell me was that she was staying with her grandpa and had gone for a walk with the dog and gotten lost. Charles was just about beside himself by the time I got that child home."

"I can imagine," said Jodi. "I'm so glad she's home safe."

"Jodi, thank you for getting involved," he told her. "I'm just glad that we found out where she belonged." He assured her that Mr. Johnson was, too.

Chapter 41

Now that the missing child issue was resolved, Jodi felt as though she could finish her painting with satisfaction. The girl hadn't been a runaway after all. She was only lost. She renamed the painting *Little Girl Lost*. It seemed much more appropriate. The old dog was the life of the painting.

"This painting has soul," said Dave when she showed it to him.

"You know, my paintings are beginning to live inside of me," she said. "Do you ever feel that way?"

"No, sweetie, I don't think I have ever felt that way about my photos. I just think you are a very sensitive artist."

"I guess maybe I am. I can still see those dried tears on her cheeks."

After learning how much *Sammy's Painting* had meant to the Parkers and certainly to herself, Jodi began to think of her work as gifts to those who bought them. In this way, she didn't experience the loss she had felt before when they were sold. School had given her a new sense of her talent. She learned that people can paint the same thing and come away with quite different results. Of course, by that same token, two viewers could also have different insights after viewing the same work. While some were moved by the slightest emotion in the painting, others only seemed to observe the color.

Take what you will from it, thought Jodi. *It is my gift to you.*

The days were growing colder, and there weren't many opportunities to paint outside. Dave suggested that they go on another camera walk to find subjects to photograph.

"That's a great idea," Jodi told him, then added with a laugh, "This time, let's not get quite so wet."

"I'm with you on that," he told her.

They walked down the beach and out to the dunes where the grasses grew the thickest. There were sea birds circling overhead and some landing in the sand. They both snapped a few shots and walked on.

"I know where there is an old shipwreck on the shoreline," she told Dave.

"Really? That would make a great subject."

"It's an old shrimper that has been there for years. Mandy and I used to play on it when we were kids."

"Lead on, skipper!" he called to her.

"Aye, aye, mate," she said with a grin.

The old boat was just up ahead. It lay half-buried in the sand. The blue paint on its hull had worn away, leaving most of its wood bare. There were two porthole windows on each side half-embedded in the sand under them.

"I bet this old boat could tell some tales," Dave said.

The long, rusted chain from the anchor still hung from the boat. The boat's hull was encrusted with barnacles. He walked around to the other side, taking pictures as he went. Jodi did the same with her camera, and they took shots at different angles.

"Between the two of us, I think we've got her covered," said Dave.

"I wonder how differently we will capture this subject," she said.

"That will be interesting to see," said Dave. "Maybe we shouldn't let each other see what we do until we are finished with it."

"I like that idea."

"We shall see what the 'Artist's Eye' reveals."

They both laughed at this one. Peter Maxwell would have enjoyed it too. It wasn't just about putting paint on canvas or snapping pictures anymore. They both were enthralled in the stories their work would tell.

"I think this will be a great subject to work on, Jodi," said Dave.

"So do I. This time of year, the sky makes the boat look so abandoned. It tells a very sad story, I would think."

After taking many shots of the boat, they decided to turn back and walk down by the water towards home. Jodi took a few more shots of the seabirds and the water. Dave was studying the shells along the way, and he walked over to the next jetty and got a few shots of those that had collected against the pilings.

"I love how the water always brings out the colors," he said.

"Yes, just like down at the lower reef," she said.

"I can't wait to go back there when it warms up some and take some underwater shots," he told her.

"Right now, I think we had better warm up some at the inn and see what Mom and Dad have for us to do."

"Yes sir, skipper sir," he teased.

Chapter 42

As the months passed, both Jodi and Dave were doing well with their artwork. Peter Maxwell had called Dave about showing some of his photographs at the gallery, and Dave was busy putting together a collection of his favorite shots and had started framing them for the showing.

"He's really good isn't he?" Alex told Susan as they had breakfast together on the back porch.

"Isn't it wonderful that Jodi found someone as talented as she is?" said Susan. "They can share their work together."

"I like the fact that they will both be showing their work in the same gallery," said Alex.

Jack had made a request that Jodi send more of her work to New York, and She had been working hard to keep sending them. She and Dave sent Peter their paintings and photographs. As always, he was very pleased. The demand for their work left them little free time. This wasn't really a problem for the couple, since both of them loved every minute they spent working on their art.

"I can't believe we are so lucky," said Jodi. "We get to earn money doing what we love."

"I know what you mean. It's awesome isn't it?" replied Dave.

Peter had mentioned to the two of them that he was hosting a showing at the Artist's Eye in a few weeks. He asked them to bring in some of their best work for display.

"I'm almost finished with my interpretation of the old shipwreck," said Jodi.

"Really? I would love to see it," Dave said.

"Not until I put the finishing touches on it."

"Okay," he laughed. "Be that way. I'll get my favorite shot of the wreck framed to take, too."

"It would be nice to have them hung side by side," she said.

"Yes, same subject, different views," he said.

"True, through different 'Artist's Eyes,'" she said with a wink.

They examined each other's works and together decided which ones to take to Atlanta. Dave thought they would have enough in about two weeks.

"That will give me time to do at least one more painting," Jodi told him.

"Great! Then we can plan to go to Atlanta two weeks from this Saturday," said Dave.

"Sounds good to me," she said.

When the mail came in the next day, there was a letter from the Waverlys. Hannah had written a thank-you note to Susan and Alex about what a great time they'd had visiting at the Sea Bird. She again told of how much enjoyment her husband had gotten from seeing his old war buddies. There was a photograph enclosed of Tom with two of his buddies saluting the flag at the reunion.

"Isn't this a great photo?" said Susan, showing the photo to Jodi.

"Yes, Mom, it really is. If you look closely, you can see tears in Mr. Waverly's eyes. These men gave so much to our country. I think it might be time to give back to them in some way."

"What do you have in mind, dear?" asked Mom.

"I think I have found my next subject to paint."

"Oh, Jodi, what a terrific idea!"

The wheels were already turning in her mind's eye for this next piece of art.

That very afternoon, Jodi set up her easel and started working on her new painting. She sketched out the three men and the flag. It was important that she show the dedication these men felt for their country. The look in their eyes would express their emotions. The lines in their faces would show the tragedies they had witnessed and the pain they had endured. She painted them in civilian clothes, because it didn't matter which branch of the service they had served in. They had each given their all. Jodi knew that everyone who served should be honored. This would be her tribute to them all.

She began working on the flag, her brushstrokes making it billow impressively in the breeze. She wanted the colors to stand out brilliantly to show that these men had come to honor what it stood for. Last but not least, she painted the tears in Tom's eyes. He stood proudly saluting *his* flag. The flag he had fought for . . . the flag he still honored. She titled the painting *The Price of Freedom*.

When she had finished, she laid down her brush and looked at the canvas. This was the first time she had done a painting in just one sitting.

I really felt this one, she thought. *I felt what I saw in their faces. I feel like I was inside my painting somehow. I've never felt like this before.*

She puzzled over this thought for a while.

I wonder if other artists feel like this. I really like this one, she thought proudly.

It was a very rewarding feeling. When she showed the painting to Dave, he just stood there and stared at it.

"What's wrong?" she asked.

Dave smiled and hugged her. "Not a thing is wrong, Jodi. It's beautiful. You told their story in their faces. Peter will not believe this one!"

"Thank you, Dave. I hope he likes it."

"You have nothing to worry about, sweetie. He'll love it. I guess I had better get cracking on my work for him. You will show me up big time."

"I love your pictures, Dave. We don't have to compete with each other."

The painting of the old wreck still needed that certain something added to it. Jodi finally decided that it had something to do with the color. The old boat had laid out in bad weather and sun for years.

"I think the color may not look worn enough. She began adding little strokes to make the paint look as though it were peeling away from the wood.

"That's more like it," she said. She was amazed at how different it looked now. "It just needed one more good storm," she laughed.

Jesse stopped by her bedroom door and looked in.

"Starting another painting?" he asked.

"No, finishing another painting," she replied.

"Can I see it?" he asked.

"Sure, come on in."

Sparky poked his nose in, too.

"Oh, I know where that is," said Jesse. "It's the old shipwreck at Carter's Cove. It looks just like that." Sparky barked at the painting. "Sparky thinks it looks like it, too," he laughed.

"Well, I'm glad that you and Sparky approve of it," said Jodi. "Let's go see if Sarah has any sugar cookies left from lunch."

"Beat you downstairs!" called Jesse as he and Sparky headed for the stairs.

While she and Jesse were eating cookies in the kitchen, Dad came in the back door.

"Got everything ready for the trip to Atlanta tomorrow?"

"We sure do. Will you need the van tomorrow?" she asked.

"No, you and Dave can use it. We can use Mom's car if we need anything."

"Want to ride along, Jesse? You might enjoy seeing the gallery."

"Can I, Dad? I finished all my homework," said Jesse.

"Sure thing, little buddy. Just let Mom know what your plans are."

"I will," he said as he and Sparky ran to tell Mom about the trip.

"Jodi, you are such a good big sister," Alex told her.

"Thanks, Dad, but it's easy when your brother is such a great kid."

"You're both great kids, sweetheart. I hope you will always know how much your Mom and I love you."

"I do, Dad," she said. "I've always felt the love. I love you both, too."

"Well, before you get me to crying, I guess I need to go rake the front yard."

"How is the leg feeling, dad? Does it still bother you?" she asked.

"It's not quite 100 percent yet, but it's getting there."

"You know, Dave and I are here to help whenever you need us," she reminded him.

"Before you know it, you two will be too famous to help out your old dad. We'll probably have to make an appointment to see you." He chuckled.

"Oh, Dad, don't be silly," she said as she gave him a big hug.

◊◊◊

It was Saturday morning, and Dave and Jodi had packed their artwork into the van. Sarah had cooked them a hefty breakfast and packed a picnic hamper with fried chicken and potato salad for their lunch. Jesse and Sparky were running around the van when Mom and Dad came out to tell them all goodbye.

"Drive safely!" called Sarah from the porch.

"We will, Sarah," Dave called back.

"We'll call you when we get there, Mom," said Jodi.

"Mind your sister, Jesse," said Dad.

"I will, Dad! Bye!" he said. "Bye, Mom and Sarah."

Sparky barked excitedly as they drove down the driveway.

"Bye, Sparky! See you tonight," called Jesse.

◊◊◊

"Come in. Come in! So good to see you again," said Peter Maxwell. He smiled at Jesse. "And who is this fine boy?"

"This is my little brother Jesse, Mr. Maxwell," said Jodi.

"Yes, yes, I do seem to remember a young man who loved model airplanes," he said.

"That's me!" said Jesse with a grin.

"I see you have quite a bit of new work here with you," said Mr. Maxwell.

"Yes we do, Peter," said Dave.

They laid out the artwork on Peter's tables so that he could look over what they had brought.

"Amazing," he said. "You are both so talented in your own way. I see here you tackled the same subject."

"The shipwreck. Yes we did," replied Jodi.

"I admire the way you caught the light on it, Dave," he said. "And the old, peeling paint, Jodi . . . You did wonders with that."

"Through different 'Artist's Eyes,'" teased Jodi.

"I see that," he laughed. His eyes traveled on to *Little Girl Lost*. "What a touching painting this is. Was this an imaginary scene?"

"No," she told him. "This really happened. I saw this little girl in our little town park and just had to paint her."

"Your animals add so much to your paintings, Jodi. This old dog is terrific."

When Peter saw *The Price of Freedom*, he stopped. He stared at it much the way Dave had when he'd seen it.

"Jodi, you have outdone yourself on this one," he told her.

"I told you he would like it," said Dave.

She smiled at him and blushed a little.

"She has no clue how good she is, Peter," said Dave.

"Jodi, if you could just stand back and listen to the comments I have heard from customers about your work," said Peter. "Maybe then you would believe in yourself more."

"Mr. Maxwell, this is the first painting I have ever done in just one sitting. It's never happened before. It all came so easily to me. I *felt* this painting. I could feel what these men felt. I just painted what I was feeling."

"You certainly captured the feelings, Jodi," Peter told her.

"Jodi, look! Look at these airplanes!" said Jesse. He had found a terrific photograph of the Blue Angels performing their air stunts.

"Look at that, Jesse!" Dave said, pointing to the colored air streams they were leaving in the air.

"Awesome!" said Jesse.

"Jesse, look who the photographer is," said Jodi.

"It says David Langley," said Jesse excitedly. "That's you, Dave! This is yours?"

"Yes it is, son," said Peter. "Your brother-in-law does some really good work, doesn't he?"

"Yes, he does. He and my big sister are a really good team!"

"You are certainly right about that, Jesse," said Peter as he gave Dave and Jodi a wink.

The trip back to Windy Point was filled with chatter. Jesse was so excited over the photographs and paintings he had seen. He was still awestruck that his own sister and her husband had their works hanging in the gallery.

"Nobody's going to believe me in school!" he said.

Chapter 43

It was becoming a routine for Jodi and Dave to make an average of two trips a month into Atlanta. Peter had a standing order for as many paintings and photographs the two could produce for him. Jodi Bennett Langley was now a frequently talked about artist in and around Atlanta. Her paintings were selling well, and some were being shipped out-of-state to other galleries.

Dave wasn't far behind with his classic black and white photographs. He had been approached the month before by a publisher with the offer to show his work in a well-known magazine. This was an exciting time for both of them. Dave was still doing ads for the newspaper, but this was much more exciting.

Alex and Susan decided to have a talk with the young couple. The four of them gathered in the living room.

"Jodi, you and Dave have been such a big help around here," said Alex. "But now, Mom and I think that you have your own futures to be concerned with. You won't have time to do your art if you are working here at the Sea Bird."

"But Dad, we can't just stop helping you and Mom!" said Jodi.

"That's right, Alex, we want to do our share," said Dave. "We can work things out so that we have time for our arts."

"Your Mom and I think maybe you and Dave should open a studio for your artwork," said Alex. "Someplace where you both can seriously put time into your work. You know Grandpa Bennett left me a small shop over on East Main Street in Windy Point. It used to be a real estate office. I think you two could do it over into a nice little studio for yourselves. What do you think?"

Jodi looked at Dave. "Would you like that, Dave?"

"Yes, I think I would, as long as you and Susan let us pay you rent," he said.

"When you start earning enough to support yourselves, then we will discuss some kind of rent," said Alex. "Deal?"

"But how will you and Mom cope with the inn without our help?" said Jodi.

"We'll do okay, Jodi," said Susan. "If we find we need some help, then we might have to hire someone, but we don't want to stand in the way of your artwork."

"That is so sweet of you, Dad and Mom," Jodi said as she hugged them both. "We won't ever forget you for this."

Dave shook Alex's hand and thanked him for their offer. Dave looked over at Jodi and grinned.

"Our own place?" he said.

"I can't wait to fix it up," said Jodi.

Now, after having heard her parents' offer, Jodi was so excited about working on the old office.

◊◊◊

Alex gave Jodi the key to the office, and she and Dave went into town to take a look at it. It had been quite a while since Jodi had been inside. The office had closed years before.

"I'm sure it will need a really good cleaning," Jodi told Dave.

"Well, it has a bathroom in the back. That's a plus," he said. "It has two big front windows. That would be good for your painting."

"And here are two large walls to display our work. Could you make a developing lab next to the bathroom?"

"I don't see why not. We just need to add a few walls back there. It would be next to the water source. I'm pretty sure we could make it all work. What should we call it? It's got to have a name."

"I'll have to get back to you on that one," Jodi told him.

They spent the rest of the afternoon sweeping and throwing out empty boxes and other clutter that had been left behind.

"I think we should put up walls for the lab first," said Dave. "Then we can have an idea of our layout for the rest of the gallery. You can start thinking about wall colors and that kind of thing. The storefront doesn't need much more than a good cleaning."

"I think you are right, Dave. We have a lot to do, though." She looked around the office. "What do you think of this for a name? 'Captured Moments Photography and Paintings by Jodi Bennett Langley and David Langley.'"

"That sounds good to me," he told her as he took her in his arms. "I'd like to capture this moment in time." He grinned and kissed her.

◊◊◊

For the next three weeks, the Langleys were at the shop every chance they could spare. They had the lights and water turned on and a phone installed. Dave's lab was ready to go. He had gotten the walls up that first week, and now they were spending most of their time painting. Jodi had chosen a soft gray because she thought it would show off their artwork well. They brought in most of their supplies and were beginning to get things arranged so they each had their own space to work.

There was a nice desk that Jodi had found at the thrift store down the street, and Dave built a few shelves and storage spaces for her paints and brushes. She brought her easel over to the front of the shop where the light would be good. Dave thought it would entice customers to come inside if they could see her working on her paintings.

"Now, all we need is to put our work on the walls," said Dave. "I guess I will have to buy one of my own ads from Ben Dawson down at the newspaper."

"You know, that's a good idea," she said. "We can have a grand opening of sorts."

Jodi hired a local sign painter to paint their shop name, and it looked beautiful hanging over the door. Alex and Susan brought Jesse down to have a look at their new shop.

"Jodi, honey, it looks very professional," said Mom.

"Good job, Dave," said Alex. "Your carpentry skills are great."

"Thanks, Alex," said Dave. "We've worked hard on it."

"It shows," said Susan.

When they felt that things were as they should be, Dave took several pictures for the ad.

"It should come out in the Saturday edition," said Dave. "We can officially open next Monday."

"I'm going to tell all of my friends about it," said Mom.

"So will I," said Jesse. "This is so neat!"

"It is kind of neat, isn't it, little buddy?" said Dad as he ruffled Jesse's hair.

They spent the rest of the afternoon putting the finishing touches on the place and storing away their supplies. When they finished, they stood out front and looked at it.

"I love it, Jodi. Don't you?" said Dave.

"I do. I can't believe we have our very own shop."

Chapter 44

Captured Moments had its grand opening, and almost all of the locals had to come and see the new shop in town. Word had traveled fast about Jodi and Dave showing their work in Windy Point. Jodi had already gained quite a reputation for her paintings over the last few years, and the newspaper had helped Dave get his name out to the public, too. Tourists were always in Windy Point, and, of course, several of them stopped by the shop to investigate.

One afternoon, while Jodi was still at the inn, a woman came in to browse the paintings.

"For some reason, these look a little familiar to me," she said.

As she studied a few more, she noticed the artist's signature on them.

"Well, what about that! I guess they do look familiar. I already own some of her work." She laughed. "This is the young woman who showed her work at the Fourth of July Celebration isn't it?"

"Yes, it is," said Dave. "That day really started her career. I'm her husband Dave Langley."

"That explains why I didn't catch the name at first," she said. "My paintings are signed 'Jodi Bennett.' I'm an interior designer, and I bought the paintings for my customers. So, you do the photography?"

"Yes, I do."

"I like the scenes on the reef. Some of my clients would enjoy these. The black and white ones would go well in an office. Very classic, I think. I'll take these two today, and I'm sure to be back again. Please tell Jodi I'm sorry that I missed her. My clients loved her work."

"I'll be sure to tell her that. Please tell your friends about our new shop, if you will."

"I certainly will," she said as she left.

◊◊◊

Soon, the shop was keeping regular hours. At least one of them was always in the shop during business days. This gave each of them time to go out on photo shoots or to find subject matter for painting. Jodi had set up an office of sorts and was keeping track of all their sales, their utilities, and the supplies they needed to purchase. They weren't getting rich, but they could at least say they were "in the black."

Dave continued doing ads for the newspaper to help make ends meet. Since they were still living at the Sea Bird, Jodi insisted that she help her mom whenever she could. This week had been a busy one at the inn. This morning, she was helping make desserts for a special gathering at the inn. They were holding a wedding reception for a local couple, and Mom and Sarah had been working hard most of the week to get everything ready. Jodi knew her mom would need her. They even had Jesse folding napkins for the guests.

The inn was beautifully decorated with ribbons, flowers, and candles. Susan was very good at this kind of thing. She was enjoying every minute of it.

"Mom, everything looks so good," said Jodi. "I know the reception will be a big success."

"Thank you, honey. I sure hope so. Dad has the yard all spruced up for the bride and groom and their wedding party. How are things going at the shop Jodi?"

"So far so good. We've had a steady stream of customers ever since the grand opening. Of course, not everyone buys, but we've made some sales and have had good feedback."

"That's very good, then. You know it doesn't happen overnight."

"We know that, Mom. We're very positive about it. You know we both love our work."

"You'll both do well, Jodi. I just know you will."

◊◊◊

The reception went off without a hitch, and attendees told Susan and Alex what a beautiful place the inn was and how much they had thoroughly enjoyed the food. Of course, Sarah had a huge part in that. The parents of the newlyweds assured the Bennetts that they would recommend the Sea Bird to all of their friends.

"I want to come and spend a weekend here next summer," said the bride's mother.

"We would be more than happy to have you stay with us," said Susan. "Just let us know when."

"Yes, leave a candle in that window right up there," laughed the bride's mother.

"We'll see what we can do," said Alex with a smile.

Chapter 45

Jodi came into the shop around ten after taking pictures for more subject matter.

"Sweetie, we had a woman in earlier today who was interested in some scenes with children," said Dave. "Do you have anything in the works?"

"I have one, but it's not quite finished," Jodi replied. "Maybe I can find time to work on it again today."

The painting was of three children on the beach, building a sandcastle. Again, it was missing that certain something that Jodi always had to include in her work. She took the painting over to her easel and looked at it. There were two little boys and a girl with sand buckets and shovels working on their castle. She decided it should have a story to go with it.

What if the two boys were trying to impress the little girl with their work? she thought. *Each trying to outdo the other?*

She would paint it so that just as one boy had gotten his part of the castle the tallest, a wave had come and washed it down. The little boy would have a crushed expression on his face. The girl would be so taken by his sadness that she would be giving him a big hug to show how much she cared. The innocence of the scene would be apparent.

I think each painting might need a story, she thought. *I'll have to remember that.*

She began work on the painting again. She gave the defeated little boy an expression that said he was on the verge of tears. He looked so sad that she wanted to hug him herself.

"Here I am, getting inside my painting again," she said. "Now I think I am the little girl."

She decided to call this one *Don't Cry, Tommy.*

"I told you that you were a sensitive artist," Dave told her when she told him how she felt about the painting.

"I can't help it, Dave. Something just comes over me."

"But, honey, you don't understand. That's what makes your paintings so special."

"Well, here's one more sensitive painting," she said.

"The lady left her number, so I'll call her and tell her you have one finished to show her. I'll tell her to come and have a look when she can."

"Paintings to order. Hmm. Sounds good to me. I got some great ideas for new ones this morning. Look at these."

"Oh, kids and kites," said Dave. "That should be a good one. These seabirds on the beach are great, too. You have a great bunch here, sweetie."

"I'm going to make a few sketches this afternoon."

"Good. Then I can go see about some new ads for the newspaper while you are here at the shop," he said.

"Okay, hon. Take your time. I have a lot to do here."

She got busy gathering her supplies by her easel.

After looking over her mornings' photographs, she decided that the seabirds would be next. She sketched out the birds. Some were hovering over the incoming waves, and others were picking at seaweed on the beach. A few birds were attracted to one on shore with a tiny fish in its beak. They seemed to be doing a kind of dance around him. She was thinking about the story again. What was happening here? Would the birds fight over the fish? Would they share it?

Okay, so now I have to think like a bird, she thought. *If I were the bird with the fish, I might feel outnumbered. It might be a good idea to show them where I got it. I think I might drop it and go back for more.*

She painted the bird with the fish dropping it in the sand just as it flew off for more.

"I think I like that idea," she told herself.

The water showed the sunrise reflecting from it. Bright streaks of the sun shot through the clouds on the horizon. Some of the seabirds were even shaded with golds and reds from the sun just as the clouds were. The painting looked as through the sea were awakening with the sun.

"I can name it *Ocean's Awakening*."

Jodi spent the rest of the afternoon working on her new painting, confident she could complete it by tomorrow. Ideas seemed to be coming to her faster than usual. She had developed more of a method to her work. First the subject, then the sketches, then the story. Finally, the brushstrokes of color themselves made the painting come to life. She smiled to herself.

"Another list, it seems. Mom and Dad can tease me all they want about my lists, but they do come in handy for me."

She had just put her brush down when Dave came back to the shop. He walked over to look at what she had been working on.

"Oh, wow!" he said. "That's great, sweetheart. I love the colors. How did you finish it so quickly?"

"You know, I really can't figure it out. Lately, these paintings just 'happen.' Is that crazy?"

"No, it's just talent, Jodi. You certainly are loaded with it."

"Thanks, honey. You know how much I love doing them."

"Well, let's close up and go see what scrumptious dinner Sarah has waiting for us tonight," he said.

She cleaned her brushes and put away her paints while Dave put his cameras away and locked up. On the way home, they discussed the new ads Dave had gotten that day. It wouldn't be long, they decided, before they would be able to pay her parents a little rent for the shop.

"It looks like we are going to make a go of it, sweetheart," said Dave.

"Yes it does, honey. Captured Moments is on its way!"

◊◊◊

Back at the Sea Bird, Alex and Susan were greeting the new guests who had just arrived. Mary Lou and Baxter Greenley were down for a week from Maine. Baxter ran his own hardware store. Mary Lou was a housewife. Their two children were both grown now, and this was the first real vacation they'd had in years.

"I can't get over your beautiful coastline here. It's so different than Maine," said Mrs. Greenley.

"Just look at this house, honey," said Baxter. "It looks so peaceful here."

"When we get your bags to your room, you can relax on the front porch with a nice glass of iced tea," said Susan.

"Oh, that sounds lovely!" replied Mary Lou. "We enjoyed the drive down, but it is a little tiring."

Dave came into the foyer as the Greenleys were heading up the stairs to their room.

"Here, Alex, let me carry those bags up for them," said Dave.

"Okay, son," said Alex. "Mr. and Mrs. Greenley, this is our son-in-law Dave. He will help you get settled in. Come back down in a bit and have that tea."

"We'll do that," said Baxter.

Jodi was in the kitchen with Susan and Sarah discussing the menu for supper. Alex came in to mention the tea for the Greenleys.

"I'll get it, Dad. You sit down," said Jodi.

"Thanks, sweetheart," he told her.

"How are things going down at the shop, dear?" asked Mom.

"Not bad, Mom. I sold two paintings this morning, and Dave sold one of his yesterday. I have another work almost finished. It should be ready tomorrow."

"You two amaze me," said Dad. "I don't know when you find the time to do your work."

"It's been working out pretty well, Dad," she said. "Dave and I trade off working in the shop, so we both get free time to look for subjects."

"You guys really work well together, don't you?" said Mom.

"That's because we understand each other," said Jodi. "We know what is important to each other. I think that's why things go so well."

"You have a good point there, sweetheart," said Dad.

The Greenleys came back downstairs. Susan showed them to the porch and brought out the iced tea.

"Thank you so much, Mrs. Bennett," said Mary Lou.

"Please, call me Susan. Make yourselves comfortable. Supper will be ready in about an hour and a half."

Jesse and Sparky ran up the front steps to the porch.

"This is our son Jesse," said Alex. "These are the Greenleys, Jesse. They've just arrived."

"Hi! This is my dog Sparky," he told them. "He thinks he owns the place."

Sparky ran over to nuzzle Mrs. Greenley's hand.

"He likes you, Mrs. Greenley."

"He knows I love dogs," she said. "We have three little poodles at home."

Sparky ran to get his ball. He came back and dropped it at Mrs. Greenley's feet.

"Let's let her rest for a while, Sparky. Okay?" said Alex. "Maybe she will play with you later."

Sparky lay down beside her.

"That's one energetic little dog," said Mr. Greenley with a smile.

"We know, we know," laughed the Bennetts.

Chapter 46

The afternoon mail arrived with a letter from Abbey Moore for Jodi. Abbey was engaged to John Forester, and they were planning a late-summer wedding so that it wouldn't interfere with school.

"How fabulous!" said Jodi to Susan. "And listen to this. She and John want to have the wedding here at the Sea Bird! She says, 'I remember how wonderful our vacation was at your inn, and we really want to have our wedding there.' Isn't that fabulous?"

Susan went to get their reservations book to see what dates they had free.

"I'll have to get in touch with her parents to discuss dates and times with them," said Susan. "I'm so happy for her!"

"John is such a sweet guy. They will make a great couple."

Jodi immediately went to call Abbey to talk about the wedding. Susan went to find Sarah to talk about food and decorations for a wedding and a reception. It was the first time that a guest at the inn had ever returned to be married here.

"Dave, I was wondering about something," said Jodi.

"What's that, sweetie?" he asked.

"Well, I know it isn't what you ordinarily take pictures of, but would you ever consider taking wedding photos?"

He thought about it for a while and then said, "You know, I've never really thought about it. I could be open to anything."

"Think about the name of our studio. Captured Moments. What greater moments to capture?"

"Were you thinking about Abbey and John's wedding?" he asked.

"Well, yes, but, of course, it would be up to them to decide. They both know you do great work."

"It would be a rather small wedding, so it might be a good one to start out with," he said. "Let me think about it before we say anything to Abbey about it. Okay?"

They agreed that they should talk about all the details that might be involved with weddings. Both of them admitted that it was exciting to think about another avenue to use Dave's talents.

Jodi thought about all the different types of moments she and Dave were capturing. Some were fun moments. Some were sad moments. Of course, there were the serious or proud moments. They were finding ways to capture scenery from wonderful vacations or special memories that would be treasured in the future. A wedding would be a beautiful memory to capture for sure.

Susan was out on the back porch when Jodi found her.

"Mom, Dave and I have an idea we want to run by you," she said.

"Sure, honey. What is it?" said Mom.

"Well, you know about Abbey's wedding. Dave and I have been talking about the wedding pictures. Do you think that Abbey and John would let Dave take their pictures for them? He's never done a wedding before, of course. It's going to be a fairly small wedding. What do you think?"

"I think that's a terrific idea, Jodi. Dave's work is always good, no matter what kind of pictures he takes. I think it's worth talking to them about."

"That's how I feel, Mom. They have both already seen what kind of work he does."

"I say, call Abbey and let her discuss it with her parents to see what they think," Mom told her.

After talking again with Dave, Jodi called Abbey to discuss the wedding pictures. They let her know that if she wasn't comfortable with this arrangement, he would completely understand. Abbey told her that she would talk to the Moores and call her back.

◊◊◊

The next morning, the phone rang at the inn. It was Abbey.

"I'm so excited, Jodi! Mama and Daddy said that if I was satisfied with Dave's work, then they were too! You know I've always loved Dave's pictures. Of course we want him to do our wedding."

"Oh, Abbey," said Jodi. "He will be so excited to hear this. I know you and John won't be disappointed."

They discussed some of the wedding details, and Jodi learned that Abbey was going to Atlanta to get her dress next week. Jodi remembered how she had felt when she and Dave had gotten married. Those were certainly unforgettable moments for her.

◊◊◊

Dave was going through wedding photographs online to get an idea of what types of shots he should take. He was getting a little like Jodi with his lists. Since many of his shots would be taken indoors, he knew he would need things like special lighting and backdrops for his subjects. This type of shooting would be different from his other work. This was an event that had to be right the first time. There was no going back for second shots.

"I can do this," he kept telling himself.

Fortunately, Jodi was there to encourage him along. She *knew* he could do it.

It was an exciting time for Abbey and John. The wedding was planned for the first week in August. This gave the couple a week for a honeymoon before school started on the last week of August. This would be the last year of school for both of them.

Life around the Sea Bird was *very* busy these last few days. It was Friday, and the Moore-Forester wedding was on Saturday.

Susan, Jodi, and Sarah had been busy making the wedding decorations and planning the food for the reception. There were to be forty guests. The ceremony was to be held in the inn's front yard with all of Alex's lovely flower beds as a backdrop. Alex and Dave had built a beautiful arbor to hold the flower garlands that Abbey had requested, and Susan had decorated two large candelabras with flower garlands to match.

The chairs were all ready to be setup. There were large ribbon bows ready to be attached anywhere they were needed. The reception was going to be in the large dining room, so Sarah and Susan had made a gorgeous table centerpiece with three large candles with beautiful, white magnolia blossoms and tiny, pink roses. Abbey had admired the magnolias the first time she had visited. Her bridal bouquet was made of pink roses and white gardenias.

The future bride and groom arrived Friday night with the Moores and the Foresters. The inn was full of excited people. Everything was as ready as it could be.

Dave gathered up all of his gear, making sure he had everything he needed. Jodi offered to make him a list so he wouldn't forget anything. He laughed at her and told her he didn't think that was necessary. He didn't tell her that he had already made his own list.

Saturday morning finally came, and everyone was having breakfast. Sarah had outdone herself with pancakes, sausage, and eggs.

"You will probably be too nervous to eat by lunchtime, so eat up now," she warned.

The ceremony would be at two that afternoon. The weather cooperated, and there was just enough of a breeze to cool things down a little.

◊◊◊

The wedding went off without a hitch. Abbey was beautiful in her long, antique lace gown. John looked at her with love in his eyes. Dave knew that was what he wanted to show through in his photographs. He caught several good shots during the ceremony. The bride and groom posed for him under the arbor, and he took a few with the preacher and the couple as they said their vows. The wedding party posed in a group as the couple stood under the arbor with the preacher.

After that, he asked Abbey and John to go inside for a few more shots. He took a few of them standing in front of the fireplace. Abbey looked at John as though she was sure she had made a good choice in this man. Dave made sure he got shots of each one of the wedding group, including John's brother who was his best man, Abbey's best friend who was her matron of honor, and John's nephew, the little ring bearer. The little girl with the flower petals was Abbey's best friend's daughter. Aunts and uncles all wanted photos for keepsakes, and Dave did his best to oblige them all. After all was said and done, he felt as though things had gone very well.

Georgeanne Moore complimented Susan and Sarah on all the food that was served.

"It wasn't just beautiful, it was delicious!" she said.

"Well that's all I wanted to hear," said Sarah with a smile.

"I love those little shrimp things," said Jesse.

"So did I," said Thomas Moore. "Of course, I haven't found anything that Sarah makes that isn't terrific! I must have gained five pounds the last time we were here."

Most of the out-of-town guests were going to stay overnight at the inn.

"Wait until you see breakfast," Thomas told them with a wink.

Abbey tossed the bouquet from the stairs, and her cousin Julie caught it. She and John would be leaving soon to go to a hotel nearby for the night. They would return to spend the rest of their honeymoon at the Sea Bird.

"I'll have to say, that went well," said Alex.

"I think so, too," replied Susan.

"Didn't Abbey look beautiful, Mom?" asked Jodi.

"Abbey is a lovely young woman," said Mom.

"John is a great guy, too," said Dave. "They are going to make two good teachers too."

Chapter 47

Dave couldn't wait to get to the shop to develop his photographs.

He set up his developing lab to work on his film, and as the photos sat in the developing solution, the images began to come through. As he watched the process, he realized that the wedding was right in front of him all over again.

Amazing! he thought. *Look at those eyes! That smile! The lighting is good, too. Oh, look at this one with the bride and groom. I can see the love in their eyes.*

This was exactly what he wanted to catch . . . the Captured Moment.

"I can't wait until Jodi sees these," he said to himself.

Later that day, when Jodi arrived at the shop, Dave practically dragged her to the back where he had the photos laid out.

"Look, sweetie," he said excitedly. "Look at these. I think I did it."

"Oh, honey! You sure did! Abbey and John will absolutely have a fit over these! I'm so proud of you, Dave. I knew you could do it."

They stood together looking over all of the shots he had taken.

"I love these of the little boy with the ring," she said. "It looks as though he was bouncing it on the pillow as he walked down the aisle."

"He was! Didn't you see it? I also got a shot of the little girl sitting in the little rocker beside the arbor. She's fast asleep!"

"*Aw*, how sweet is that? Abbey will love these."

"I'll try to have some proofs ready for them to see when they get back tomorrow," said Dave.

◊◊◊

John and Abbey were back at the Sea Bird by Sunday night. By then, the other guests had all returned home. At the dinner table that night, everyone was talking about how nice the wedding had been. When Dave mentioned the wedding pictures, Abbey couldn't wait to see them. After the table had been cleared, they all gathered around to see the proofs Dave had made.

"Oh, Dave!" said Abbey. "These are beautiful! Look, honey, there is the little flower girl who fell asleep! That's so cute."

"We could not have asked for anything better than these, Dave," said John. "These are awesome!"

"You really captured our moment," said Abbey. "I'm so glad that we could be your first wedding."

"So am I, Abbey. I'm glad that it could be with friends we already knew," said Dave.

Jodi and Abbey had time during their visit to catch up on old times together.

"Jodi, you won't believe where John and I are going to be living when we go back to Atlanta," Abbey said.

"Is it . . . could it be our apartment?" Jodi ventured a guess.

"*Yes*! We thought it would be perfect for us!"

"Oh, Abbey, sometimes I miss those days. I loved that place."

"But look at you now, Jodi . . . Married to a great guy and with a real business and a shop of your own. How could it get any better?"

"I'm not sure it can get any better," Jodi said. "My wish for you and John is that you will be as happy together as we are."

"Thank you, Jodi. That's such a sweet thing to wish for us."

◊◊◊

The newlyweds spent lots of hours walking on the beach together. They watched sunrises and sunsets from the beach and from the front porch.

"John I love this place," said Abbey. "I hope we can come back here again, don't you?"

"Yes, I do. Maybe we can spend our first anniversary here," he told her.

"Sounds good to me," she told him.

They sat cuddled up on the porch swing watching as the sun slowly slipped below the horizon. Dave slipped up behind them and took a picture of their silhouettes.

"Another captured moment," he laughed.

"Dave!" cried Abbey.

"That's okay, honey. I don't mind him capturing our moments like this one," John said as he kissed her.

◊◊◊

That night, while Dave and Jodi lay in bed, they talked about what an unexpected surprise it was for Dave to have gotten involved in wedding photography.

"You know, I really enjoyed doing that," he told her. "I wasn't sure if it would come easily to me, but I can see now that I just let it happen and captured what I saw on film."

"That's almost what I feel when I am painting. I just paint what I feel." She laughed and added, "Maybe we are what Abbey used to call us."

"What did she call us?" he asked.

"'Two peas in a pod,'" she laughed.

"Maybe she was right," he said. "Besides," he teased, "I like peas." He tickled her in the ribs.

"Silly!" she said and kissed him.

"I love you, Mrs. Langley," he said as he pulled her close to him.

"I love you too, Mr. Langley."

"You know, Abbey and I talked today about how happy you and I are. She said, how could it get any better?"

"Yes, and? How could it get any better?"

"I'll let you guess," she teased.

"Well, let me see . . ." said Dave. "What if . . . ? What if we had a little Langley?"

"I think that would be *perfect!*" she said as she snuggled closer.

"Let's see if we can work on that tonight," he snickered.

"Turn out the light, Dave," she said as she wrapped her arms around him.

Chapter 48

Jesse and Dave were in the backyard throwing the football back and forth while Sparky ran from one to the other trying to catch it.

"Go out for a pass, Sparky!" yelled Dave.

He threw the ball and, believe it or not, Sparky caught it.

"Great job, Sparky!" said Jesse. "Can you believe that?"

"With that dog? I can believe just about anything," said Dave.

They came in the back door just as Alex arrived with the mail. He went into the kitchen where Susan and Jodi were working.

"There's a letter here from Abbey and John, Jodi," he said as he handed her the letter.

"Thanks, Dad," she said as she opened it. After reading it, she reported, "Abbey says that they just had exams, and both did well on them. She also says that married life is treating them very well. They are loving the little apartment, and they just got a little dog."

"That's cool," said Jesse.

"She says to tell you that he looks a lot like Sparky but not quite as smart."

Sparky heard his name and barked at him.

"Yes, we know you are smart, Sparky," Jesse told him.

"Well, I have to get going. I have an appointment for a photo shoot in Windy Point," said Dave. "It's a young man who is graduating from college this spring."

"Nice going, Dave," said Alex. "Before long, you will be taking everyone's picture."

"I sure hope so, Alex."

◊◊◊

Later that morning, Jodi drove to the shop to work on a painting.

"I'm going out to the Lower Reef again, sweetie," Dave told her.

"Ok, hon. I think I'll work on my painting with the kites," she said.

"Catch you later," he said as he picked up his camera bag.

She put the painting on the easel and looked at it. She had only gotten the first stages of it done. There were four children in the picture. Each had a kite but only three of them were flying. The fourth little boy was sitting on the ground holding his. The string was all tangled up into a huge knot.

"I think I will give this boy a really hopeless look," she told herself.

She was thinking about a story for this painting.

The older boy is his brother, and he will give his kite to the younger one and try to fix the string for him.

The little boy was looking towards his brother with a "help me" look on his face. The big brother was looking back towards him. In her mind, Jodi could just see the big brother handing the younger one his kite and attempting to untangle the string for him.

"I'll call this one *My Brother's Keeper*."

The painting began to take shape. She added in the bright colors of the kites. She made the tails of the kites swirl to show their movement. The clothing was next. The children's faces made it real.

"You are such a good brother," she told the older boy as she painted him. "Your little brother will always look up to you."

Before she knew it, the scene had come alive. The painting conveyed the bond between the two brothers. She could almost imagine the two boys walking home with smiles on their faces.

When Dave got back to the shop, she told him about her painting.

"You know, I love painting landscapes and still life, but my people speak to me," she said. "I can feel what they feel."

"No, Jodi, *you* put the feelings into your people. *You* make them alive," said Dave. "Otherwise, they are just paint on canvas."

"I never thought about it that way," she said. "I think I will go out for a while with my camera. I need some new subjects to work on. I'll walk the shoreline this time."

"I got some good shots at the reef this morning," he told her.

"I'm going to stop by the Sand Dollar to get a sandwich first. Can I bring you back anything?" she asked.

"No, I grabbed a bite before I got back to the shop."

She gathered up her camera and a lightweight jacket. "I'll see you in an hour or two."

"See you, sweetie," he called out from the back.

◊◊◊

Mandy saw Jodi come into the sandwich shop.

"Hey there, kiddo!" said Mandy. "How are you doing?"

"Hey, Mandy," said Jodi. "I know I haven't seen you in a while. We are staying pretty busy here lately."

"So I hear. I heard the wedding was beautiful."

"It was. Abbey made a lovely bride. I got a letter from her the other day. They are both doing really great."

"That's good to hear. I liked Abbey a lot."

"I need a chicken salad sandwich to go and a sweet tea," Jodi told her. "I'm going out on a camera run for more subject matter."

"If you can wait for a few minutes I can walk with you for a while. We aren't that busy today."

"Sure! We haven't had time to talk much lately."

Mandy rang up her last customer, and together, they walked down towards the shoreline.

"I have something to tell you, Jodi," Mandy said.

"What's that?" Jodi asked.

"I've met a really great guy since I last saw you. He's just moved here from South Carolina. We've had a few dates, and I really like him."

"Now that's good news, Mandy. I knew it was just a matter of time until you would find someone. Tell me all about him."

"Well, his name is Gordon Chriswell. He has blond hair and the prettiest green eyes you've ever seen. He's twenty-one years old and works at Mobley's Hardware. He's their nephew. I think he might be training to take over the store when the Mobleys retire. You know they don't have any sons of their own. Their son-in-law has his own business in real estate, so he wouldn't be interested."

"Awesome, Mandy. It sounds like *you* have been busy, too," she laughed.

They walked over to one of the sand dunes and sat down. Jodi opened up her sandwich.

"I'm so hungry," she said. "Sarah packed me a sandwich for work, but I'm hungry all over again."

She drank her tea while they talked about what was going on around Windy Point.

"I should be heading back, Jodi," said Mandy. "I'm so glad we got to spend some time together."

"So am I. We'll have to try to get together more often."

"Catch you later," Mandy said as she left to return to the Dollar.

Jodi walked on down the beach and took some shots along the way. She watched a few children playing along the water's edge. They were trying to race the waves back to the shore. They were giggling while they ran, and it was a cute scene. She also saw a dog trying to dig up sand fiddlers on the beach. She took shots all along the trip back to the shop.

"Hey, hon," she said as she came in the door. "I spent a little time with Mandy while I was out. She's got a new boyfriend."

"Ah, good news!" Dave replied.

"He's the Mobley's nephew Gordon Chriswell."

"Hey, I think I met him the other day at their store. Seems like a nice enough guy," said Dave.

"I hope this works out for her. I feel as though I have kind of left Mandy out of things."

"She'll be fine, Jodi."

"Are there any snacks here? I'm hungry."

"I don't think so. Didn't you get a sandwich when you left?"

"Yes, but it has worn off already," she said.

"Any luck with the camera shots?" Dave asked.

"Yes, I got a few cute ones on the beach. Kids and dogs. My favorite subjects." She smiled.

When the two of them got back to the inn late that afternoon, Jodi headed straight for the kitchen.

"Sarah, do you have anything I can snack on?"

"There is some cheese and crackers if you would like that," Sarah told her.

Jodi poured herself a glass of milk, grabbed up a pack of crackers and a few slices of cheese, and headed for the front porch rocker.

"Oh, there you are," Dave said. "I wondered where you had gotten to."

"I had to find something to eat. I was famished," she said. "Want some?"

"No thanks. I'll just wait for supper," he told her. "I think I will look Jesse up for a quick game of catch before we eat."

"He'll love that, hon," she told him.

◊◊◊

Dave went through the house and met Alex coming in the back door.

"Is Jesse around?" asked Dave. "I wondered if he would like to play catch for a while."

"He's in the back yard. We've been cleaning up the firepit, and I asked him to put the tools away for me," said Alex.

"Anything I can help you with, Alex?"

"No, Dave. You know, Jesse is getting big enough to do quite a bit around here."

"Okay, just thought I would ask. I'll see if he has finished up yet."

When Alex came into the kitchen to wash up, he mentioned to Susan that Dave was still asking to help out.

"You know he wants to help whenever he can, Alex," she said. It won't hurt to let him think we still need him."

"My leg is back to normal now, and Jesse has been a big help to me," said Alex. "I don't want Dave to feel obligated to stay here with us."

"I think he just wants to let us know that he is grateful to us for helping them get started," said Susan. "He's really a great son-in-law."

Sarah had a nice pot roast for supper served with hot homemade biscuits.

"This looks terrific, Sarah," said Jodi. "I'm starved."

"I made apple pie for dessert," said Sarah.

"All my favorites," said Jodi.

There were three other guests staying at the inn. After supper, they wandered into the living room. It was beginning to cool off a little at night, so Alex had started a fire.

"Isn't this homey?" said Mrs. Jessup.

"I love a good fire," said her husband George.

The Jessups had been at the inn for a few days now. George was a retired professor from Athens. His wife had been a school teacher.

"You have such a beautiful home here, Susan," Polly Jessup told her.

"We were very fortunate to have inherited it from Alex's parents," Susan told her. "They ran the inn before we did."

"It's so peaceful here, not at all like the places we've stayed at before," said George. "When we were in town today, we noticed that your daughter and her husband have a shop there."

"Oh, yes, they sure do. Did you go inside?" asked Alex.

"We didn't," said Polly. "We were a little rushed today, but I think we will the next time we go to Windy Point."

"They both do some amazing art," said Susan. "You really should see their work before you go."

"I was there on Tuesday," said Miss Mayweather, a librarian visiting from Augusta. "They have some lovely paintings and photographs there. They really are a talented young couple."

"If you would like a souvenir of the Sea Bird, there is a beautiful painting done of the beach right here," said Miss Mayweather.

"Well, now I know we have to go," said Polly.

"You won't regret it," said Mrs. Mayweather.

Chapter 49

Captured Moments was really getting busy these days. Visitors recommended it to their friends, and word of mouth was really paying off. The ad Dave had placed in the newspaper was helping, too.

"I think you should display some of your wedding shots in the front window, hon," Jodi told him. "Some people may not have heard yet that you are doing weddings now."

"That might be a good idea, sweetie," he said. "I'll pick some out today. You can show some of yours in the other window, too."

"I'll finish up this one with the kites today and use it for the window display."

"Awesome! I like that one."

Jodi began getting out her brushes and paints to work on the painting. There wasn't a lot left to do with the work. She was just doing the final touches on it. She opened up a few tubes of paint and the chemicals to clean her brushes. She hadn't even started to paint when suddenly she realized that she was getting lightheaded.

"Wow, that's never happened before," she said.

"What, sweetie? Did you say something?" asked Dave.

"Yeah, I just got dizzy from smelling my supplies," she told him.

"Why don't you go out front for a sec and get some fresh air?" he suggested.

"I think I will," she replied.

Jodi stood outside the door for a few minutes in the sunshine. It seemed to clear her head, so she went back inside.

"Do you feel better now?" Dave asked.

"Yeah, I do, but I really don't feel like painting now," she told him.

"Why don't you go on home and rest awhile? I'll put your things away for you."

"That's sweet of you, Dave. I might come back later this afternoon."

"Don't worry about that, Jodi. You do look a little pale today."

Jodi took the car and drove back to the inn. By the time she got there, all she could think of was taking a nice, long nap.

"Everything okay, honey?" said Susan.

"Not really, Mom. I felt a little dizzy at work when I opened my paints and things. Now all I want to do is sleep."

"You go take yourself a good nap. Let me know if you need anything."

"Thanks, Mom. I will."

◊◊◊

When Dave got home that afternoon, Jodi was still asleep.

"Is she okay?" Dave asked Susan. "She looked awfully pale to me this morning."

"I think she just needed a good rest," Susan told him.

When Susan went back into the kitchen, Sarah looked at her and said, "Uh-huh," with a wink at Susan.

After an hour had passed, Jodi came downstairs into the living room.

"Jodi, sweetie, do you feel better now?" Dave asked her.

"Yes, hon. I guess I was a little overtired or something. I want to see if Sarah has something I can munch on before supper. I didn't eat any lunch. I need to settle my stomach."

She went into the kitchen to see what she could find.

"Feeling better, Jodi?" asked Sarah.

"Yes, I think I'm okay now. Do you have anything to settle an empty stomach?"

"What about some saltines? They usually work."

"Jodi, you do still look a little pale to me," said Mom. "You aren't running a fever are you?"

"I don't think so," she said. "I was feeling fine until I smelled those paints and chemicals this morning."

"Uh-huh," said Sarah.

"What do you mean, 'uh-huh,' Sarah?" she asked.

"Nothing, nothing at all," Sarah said as she gave Susan a knowing look and left the kitchen.

"Jodi, tell me, honey, when did you have your last cycle?" Mom asked.

"What? Oh, that. I'm a little late, but I thought it might be because we've have been so busy."

"I think you might think about going to see Doc Stanton and let him check you out."

"Really? Are you thinking I might be pregnant?" Jodi asked in surprise.

"Well, it's always a possibility," said Mom with a little smile on her face.

"Wow! I never even thought about that. I'll go by his office in the morning before I go into the shop."

"I think that's a good idea," said Mom.

"Don't say anything to Dave about this," said Jodi. "If it's true, I want to surprise him with the news."

"Mum's the word," said Mom.

For the rest of the night, Jodi felt like the cat that had swallowed the canary. Every time she looked at Dave, she had to hold back a grin.

◊◊◊

The next morning, Dave and Jodi left for the shop early. Jodi was feeling much better. After they got inside, she told Dave that she had an errand to run first.

"I shouldn't be too long, hon," she said.

She only had a short distance to walk to Doc Stanton's office around the corner. Since it was still early, the doctor's office said they could see her right away.

"What seems to be the problem, Miss Jodi?" asked Doc Stanton.

"Well," said Jodi. "I want to know if I might be pregnant."

After asking her a few questions, the nurse took her to the examination room. The doctor looked her over and did a checkup on her.

"Well, my little Miss Jodi, I think you just might be right about that," said the doctor. "It's still early, but I believe you may be about two months pregnant."

"Are you serious? Oh, Dave will be thrilled with this!"

"Let's do a test to be sure before you go yelling to the hills. Okay?" he said.

After about fifteen minutes the nurse came back in with the results.

"You're going to be a mom, Jodi," she said.

At this point, Jodi burst into tears.

"You will make a very good mother, Jodi," Doc told her. "I've always known that, dear."

She hugged his neck. Doc Stanton had delivered Jodi, so she had known him all of her life.

When Jodi got back to the shop, she couldn't stand it any longer. Dave looked up at her when she came in the door. The good news was written all over her face.

"*We are going to have a baby!*"

Chapter 50

Life around the Sea Bird now was all about the news of the baby. Susan, Jodi, and Sarah were so excited about creating a nursery for the new arrival, and Dave wanted to build the crib for his new baby. There was a rather large linen closet next to their bedroom. Alex said he would add a new window and start painting the new room. They were sure this would make an ideal nursery.

Jesse was thrilled at the thought of becoming an uncle. And Sparky? Well, Sparky was just excited because everyone else was excited.

The expectant parents were sitting in front of the fire.

"Sweetheart, nothing could make me any happier," Dave told Jodi.

"I'm so happy, Dave. This baby will make our lives complete."

They sat there just holding each other, enjoying the fire.

"Look at that," said Sarah. "Did you ever see a happier couple?"

"Just think, Sarah, Alex and I are going to be grandparents!" said Susan.

They could not wait for the new baby to arrive.

◊◊◊

After getting through the next few weeks, Jodi was beginning to feel stronger. Thank goodness the queasy stomach was a thing of the past.

A little baby bump was beginning to grow. She looked at herself in the mirror every chance she got to see how big it was.

She was thrilled at the thought of being a new mom. The baby was to be born in the spring.

She and Susan went to town to shop for maternity clothes.

"Dave will make a terrific dad," she told Mom.

"I'm sure he will," said Susan. "I see how he has always spent time with Jesse. I don't care if it is a girl or a boy.

"I just love children so much, it doesn't matter at all," said Jodi.

◊◊◊

Jodi was now able to resume her painting. The smells of paints and chemicals no longer made her sick. She had finally completed the painting with the kites, and it had only been on display in the window for a week before it sold. The man who bought it said that it reminded him of him and his big brother. Their father had died when they were young, and the older brother had always protected him.

"He always *was* my keeper," he told her. "That kind of bond never dies."

She smiled. "I'm so glad that you are the one buying this painting. I feel as though it has a good home."

Dave had two weddings on his calendar. He was becoming more and more popular after people had seen the work he had done for Abbey and John. He had realized how much he enjoyed being a part of such a special moment in people's lives.

Jodi had kept in touch with Jack Parker and Peter Maxwell and still sent the occasional painting or photo to their galleries. Captured Moments had made a real name for itself, and they needed most of their artwork for their own sales. Orders were coming in from out of state after buyers had seen their work in the other galleries.

The painting Jodi was working on now was from a photo she had taken about a month ago. She was walking through town and saw an old couple sitting in the park. The old man was helping his wife to sit down on the bench. It was clear by his movement that he was not in very good shape himself, yet he was still devoted to helping her first. The love and appreciation for him showed in her eyes. It was such a touching scene to witness. She called the painted *Devotion*.

She worked on the faces to show the feeling she read into the painting. The bent back of the old man and the lines of age in their faces were all part of it. She painted in the old, worn wedding rings on their hands.

Together forever, she thought.

"This will be Dave and me in our old age," she said to herself.

◊◊◊

"Thanksgiving will be here before we know it," said Sarah.

"I think I could be the turkey this year," said Jodi as she rubbed her growing belly.

"You'll have to let that turkey roast a little longer," laughed Sarah.

"Don't worry. It will be here before you know it," said Mom.

"I know, Mom, but I'm beginning to feel a little awkward."

"All part of the deal," said Dad.

"It's worth it," said Jodi as she felt the baby kick her.

This part of the pregnancy fascinated her. She loved feeling the baby move inside her. As Dave came into the room, she reached for his hand and held it against her belly.

"Do you feel that?" she asked.

"Wow, I do feel that!" he said. "That's so awesome, sweetie. Is that our little football player?"

"It could be our little ballerina," she said with a grin.

"Time will tell," said Sarah.

Jodi went upstairs into the new nursery. She had gotten into the habit of folding and refolding the little clothing they had bought for the baby.

"These are so sweet. I can't wait to hold you, little one," she said as she rubbed her belly.

Chapter 51

It was Thanksgiving Day, and the folks at the inn were impatient to taste the delicious foods they had been smelling for hours. Susan's parents, the Gardners, had gotten there the night before. Uncle Frank had driven them up again.

"Look at our precious, little mother-to-be," said Olive as she lovingly rubbed Jodi's belly.

"Are you feeling okay?" said George.

"Yes, Grandpa," said Jodi. "Aside from feeling like a small whale, I feel fine."

Uncle Frank gave her a big hug, and he shook hands with Dave.

"We think she might have swallowed a watermelon," Jesse said with a grin.

"Jesse!" said Mom. "That's not very nice."

"I'm sorry, Jodi. I was only teasing you," said Jesse.

"It's okay, buddy. It does look a little like that, doesn't it?" said Jodi.

She would have ruffled his hair, but Jesse was getting a little particular about it these days. He had turned thirteen this past summer. She couldn't believe that her little brother was already a teenager.

Albert and Mona Hamilton had returned to the Sea Bird for the holiday.

"It's so much easier to enjoy Sarah and Susan's cooking, especially when it's just the two of us," said Mona.

"Congratulations on the new expected arrival, my boy," said Albert as he patted Dave on the back.

"Thank you, sir," said Dave. "We are very happy about it."

"We have two sons, but they live so far away we don't get to see much of them," said Mona. "We're hoping they may make it for Christmas this year."

"If they can't, feel free to come back to the Sea Bird and spend it with us," said Alex.

"We might just do that," said Albert.

The supper table that night was all aglow with Susan's candles and another beautiful centerpiece. Everyone was discussing their future plans and, of course, the wonderful meal they were enjoying. Alex stood for the Thanksgiving Blessing.

"Father, we have so very much to be thankful for this year," he said. "Thank you for our lovely family and our wonderful guests who chose to spend this time with us. Thank you for our health and well-being. Bless us all throughout this coming year. And Lord, thank you for the blessing of our new grandchild to be."

"*Amen!*" said everyone.

Chapter 52

The days at the shop had been very busy. Both Jodi and Dave had to share the responsibility of keeping track of orders for more paintings and photographs and the ordering of more supplies for the shop. It was a full day for both of them. Christmas was only two weeks away, and people were ordering family portraits. Dave already had several photo shoots completed, but there were still more to be done. He and Jodi had designed a beautiful background for their sittings. The portrait was done with a large, paned window in front of the family. It looked as though the portrait had been taken from outside the house looking in at the family. It was a very unusual effect, and Jodi loved it. She felt as though this would be talked about for years.

"We needed something 'out-of-the-box,'" she said.

Jodi had also done a family portrait for Christmas featuring some parents, a little girl, an older boy, and a small puppy. This was going to be one of her favorites. The puppy she painted was squirming just as the real dog had done. She had caught him in action. The little girl had her two front teeth missing, and the boy was tugging at her pigtail. This painting was so natural. It was going to be a *real* family. She wondered if when they looked back on this, years from now, they would say, "That's us!"

Each one of the family members was doing some sneaking around to get their shopping done. There were lots of whispers behind closed doors to keep all of their secrets. Jodi had found the perfect gift for Dave: a developing lab. She had done an online search and ordered it to surprise him. It wasn't new, but it had all the newest features. It would be much more efficient than the one he had been using.

◊◊◊

Dave had gone Christmas shopping, and he knew what he had gotten for Jodi would thrill her.

"Susan, would you mind wrapping something for me?" he asked.

"Sure, Dave, what do you have?"

"It's for Jodi. Please don't let on that I got this for her," he said, beaming. He handed her a tiny ring box. It was a beautiful diamond ring with tiny diamonds set on each side.

She opened it and said, "Oh, Dave! It's gorgeous!"

"I couldn't afford a real ring when we got married, so I've been saving up to buy her this one."

"She will absolutely love it," said Susan. She gave him a kiss on the cheek. "You are such a good husband to her, Dave."

"I want you to wrap it in a larger box so she can't guess what it is ahead of time," he said.

"Smart thinking, Dave. I'll keep her guessing," she laughed.

◊◊◊

Christmas morning came at last. Everyone was gathered around the beautifully decorated tree. Sarah had already served the homemade sweet rolls, coffee, and juice.

"Jesse, why don't you play the mailman and pass out the gifts for us?" said Mom.

"Sure thing, Mom! Here's one for Mom," he said as he handed Susan a beautifully wrapped package.

"Oh, Jodi! It's lovely! I love the color, too," she said as she took out the hand-knitted sweater.

"Here's one for Dave from me," said Jesse.

Dave opened the package and found a sweatshirt for the football team he loved.

"Thanks, buddy," he said. "Maybe I can wear this to one of their games. Sarah, here's one for you."

Sarah unwrapped hers to find a terrific new cookbook from Susan.

"This is the one I have been reading about," said Sarah. "Thank you so much, Susan. I love it."

"Dad, this is for you from Mom," said Jesse.

Alex unwrapped a heavy box that contained a new drill and bit set.

"I've been looking at these, honey," said Alex. "Thank you!"

"Jesse, open one for yourself," said Jodi.

"Okay, here's one to me from Mom and Dad," he said.

It was a big box. Inside was a model of the Stealth Fighter Jet. He had been drooling over this one for months.

"Dave, here's one to you from Jodi," Jesse told him.

When Dave opened the box he gave her a huge hug. "Oh, sweetie, if you only knew how much I wanted this!" He kissed her. "Here is mine to you, Jodi," he said as he handed her his gift.

Jodi slowly tore the paper off. Inside the box, she found another box. She gave him a strange look. Inside the next box, she found yet another box.

"What is this?" she laughed.

When she finally got to the last box, she realized what it was. She slowly tore off the paper. When she opened the tiny box, she burst into tears.

"Dave, oh, honey! It's beautiful!" She hugged his neck and kissed him.

"I told you someday I would get you a real ring," he told her. "Today is the day. I love you, sweetheart."

"How sweet!" said everyone together.

"What a great Christmas this has been," said Alex.

Everyone agreed that it was the best they had ever had.

Chapter 53

The New Year was bringing many changes to the Langley's lives.

Captured Moments was becoming well-known all around the area for great paintings and photography work. It was wonderful to hear customers come into the shop and talk about how much they had heard about the Langley's work. Alex had told them more than once that satisfied customers tell other people about the kind of service you provide. This was true concerning most any kind of service, including the inn. Jodi and Dave had even talked about enlarging their shop to include a separate room just for photo shoots. Dave would be able to do most of the work himself. Alex, of course, had offered his services, too. Their heads were filled with new ideas for the business.

It was on one of these busy mornings that the shop had some very special visitors arrive: the Parkers from New York.

"How wonderful to see you, Mr. and Mrs. Parker!" said Jodi. "What brings you to Windy Point?"

"We came to see *you!*" Jack told her. "We have heard from our clients that you and Dave are doing a great job in your new shop. We had to come and see for ourselves."

"Well, come right in and see what we are doing."

When Jodi stepped out from behind the desk, Meredith noticed the *very* obvious change in her.

"Look at you!" said Meredith. "We hadn't heard *that* news!"

"Congratulations, Jodi," said Jack.

"Thank you, Jack," said Jodi. "We are so excited over it. How is your little Samantha doing?"

"Oh, she's all over the place now," Jack said, beaming. "She started walking a few months ago, and there is no stopping her."

"That's so wonderful," said Jodi. "Ours is due in April."

The Parkers walked around the shop admiring the beautiful paintings and photography.

"I see Dave is doing wedding shots," said Jack. "He's done such a good job on these. Captured Moments is the perfect name for your shop. You both certainly do capture them."

"Jack, I have you to thank for encouraging me to show my work that summer," said Jodi. "I don't think I would have come this far if it hadn't been for you."

"You only needed to have a little faith in yourself. That's all it took. The talent was already there."

"I can see that you are continually improving, Jodi," said Meredith. "Your paintings have so much feeling in them."

"I think I am beginning to live inside them while I paint," laughed Jodi.

"Every artist has their own method of accomplishing what they want their viewer to see," said Jack. "If 'living in the painting' is what it takes for you . . . then so be it."

Meredith stood looking at the painting of the old couple in the park. "I am drawn to this one, Jack. It looks like my grandparents."

"Wrap it up, Jodi," he said with a grin.

She carefully wrapped the painting *Devotion* for the Parkers. She knew they would love it. She always loved to send her paintings to a good home. It was almost like sending her child out into the world.

"Well, Mrs. Langley, we wish you the very best on your new baby," said Jack, "and, of course, with your shop. We are both very impressed with what you and Dave have done here."

"I'm so sorry that Dave wasn't here to see you again," Jodi said.

"Give him our best," Jack told her. "We will try to come back again whenever we can."

"Please do. It was great to see you again."

After they had gone, she sat thinking about what she should paint next. She would have to go on another camera run when Dave got back to the shop. The scenery around Windy Point was beginning to show signs of an early spring. The weather was warming up just a bit, so she should see more people out and about.

It should be a good time to look for new subject matter, Jodi thought.

"Honey, you will never guess who was just here!" she said as Dave came in the door.

"I give. Who?"

"Jack and Meredith Parker!"

"No kidding! What brought them way down here?"

She told him what Jack had said about his clients raving over the shop and their work.

"That's always good to hear," Dave said.

"Meredith even bought one of my paintings." Dave looked around the room. "I see grandma and grandpa are gone. Did they buy that one?"

"Yes, she loved *Devotion.* She said it looked like her grandparents."

"Good job, sweetie!" he told her.

He gave her a hug but it was awkward to do so without disturbing the baby.

"This is getting harder to do, isn't it?" she laughed.

"Yes, it is, but it won't be too much longer, sweetie."

She told him she was leaving to do a subject matter search.

"Okay, Jodi, be careful you don't go too far," he said protectively.

"I won't go far, honey."

She blew him a kiss goodbye as she gathered up her gear.

After walking a short distance down the block, a thought came to her.

Windy Point itself might be a good subject. I could do a shot taken down the street showing some of these quaint, little shops along the way. I think the people living here would love that.

She walked up and down the street taking pictures all along the way. There was the bakery, the barber shop, the grocery, the drug store, Doc Stanton's, and, of course, their own shop. She walked back in the other direction to take pictures of the same stores from different angles. The lighting would be different that way too.

People who worked in some of these shops noticed her taking pictures, and a few came out to ask her what she was up to.

"You'll just have to wait and see," she told them with a wink and a smile.

"I'm sure it will be something good," said one.

"Time will tell," she said.

Further down the street, she noticed a young mother trying to get two little children to cooperate with her while she carried her shopping bags. She could see it had been a struggle. The mother was trying her best to keep her patience with them. Jodi took a few shots and then headed back to the shop.

"Let's go to the Dollar and get some lunch," said Dave when she got back.

"That's a great idea," Jodi replied. "I'm starved. I'll get to see Mandy again, too."

Mandy was clearing a table when they got to the Sand Dollar.

"What can I get you, little mama?" Mandy teased.

"Hey, Mandy. How about a horse or two?" she laughed.

"I think we will both have a hamburger and fries," said Dave. "You can hold the horses for now." He winked.

"You look great, Jodi," said Mandy. "Are you feeling good?"

"Yes, I am. I was queasy at first, but after that passed I've been doing fine."

"Glad to hear that," said Mandy. "I'll be back in a few minutes with your food."

Dave looked around the room. "See the guy over at the counter? That's Gordon Chriswell, the Mobleys' nephew. That's Mandy's new boyfriend."

"*Oh . . .*" **said Jodi. "I wonder if she will say anything about him to us," she laughed.**

Mandy brought their order out and placed it on the table.

"Jodi, there's someone I want you to meet," she said. "Gordon, come here a sec."

The young man at the counter got up and walked over.

"This is my best friend Jodi and her husband Dave," said Mandy. "Jodi, Dave, this is Gordon Chriswell, my boyfriend."

"Oh, hey! I've heard some things about you, Jodi," Gordon said. "Didn't I meet you the other day at the hardware store, Dave?"

"Yes, you did. Hello again."

"Mandy has told me a lot about you too, Gordon. It's nice to finally put a face to a name," said Jodi.

"Jodi and I have been friends since we were little kids," said Mandy.

"Yeah, about a hundred years ago," laughed Jodi.

After they had eaten, Dave and Jodi walked back to the shop. They both agreed that Gordon was a good choice for Mandy, which made Jodi happy.

As they passed the little shops along the way, Jodi again thought about her next painting. There was Mr. Mobley in front of the hardware, sweeping the sidewalk. Mrs. Burdock was cleaning the front window of her bakery, and she noticed the barber pole.

That all has to be part of it, she thought.

She couldn't wait to start her sketches. She would have to think of a good name for this piece.

At the shop Jodi, went straight to her easel. She looked at her pictures, then started her sketches. By the time she and Dave were ready to go home, she knew how it would all look on canvas. This one would be called *Welcome to Windy Point.*

Chapter 54

The baby's room was almost finished now. The new window allowed so much more sunlight into the room. They had chosen a soft yellow for the walls, and Jodi and her Mom had enjoyed picking out the new bedding for the beautiful, white crib Dave had built for the baby. Jodi was so proud of her husband. He had spent a great deal of his spare time building this crib. He had even carved a tiny seagull on the headboard.

When Susan came in, she laughed and said, "Jodi, I think if you keep folding those little clothes, they will be worn out by the time the baby gets here."

"I know, Mom, but they are *so* sweet! I just love handling them."

"Sarah said to tell you that you won't need to buy a rocker for the room. She wants you to have the one her grandmother gave her."

"Oh, Mom! That is so sweet of her to offer that to us."

"I have some pretty, yellow fabric to make new cushions for it," Susan told her.

"All we need now is the baby," said Jodi happily.

"Well, that *is* the reason for the room," laughed Mom.

When they hugged each other, the baby gave a sharp kick.

"I think your little one is growing impatient in there," said Mom.

"Are you girls upstairs?" called Alex.

"We are in the baby's room!" called Susan.

"I thought I would find you here," he said as he came in. "The room looks great, doesn't it?"

"It's perfect, Dad," said Jodi.

"I have something to show you two," said Alex. "Can you come outside for a little while?"

Susan and Jodi followed him out into the front yard.

"What is it, honey?" asked Susan.

"Look over here," he said, pointing to his flowerbeds.

Sparky ran over to see what they were looking at. There, along the edges of the bed, were tiny green sprouts just popping their heads through the dirt.

"The flowers that Dave and Jesse planted are coming up," said Alex. "And you, Mr. Sparky, are *not* to dig them up. It looks like spring might be a little early this year."

"I like the thought of that, Dad," said Jodi. "I'm a little tired of wearing my coat over this big belly of mine."

"Aw, Sweetheart it will come soon enough," said Dad.

"You only have another few weeks to go," said Mom.

"I'm counting them down, Mom," she said.

◊◊◊

Jodi and Dave got right to work when they arrived at the shop. Jodi got out her sketches of the shops. This one excited her. She hadn't done a painting quite like this one before. She wanted the colors to be bright enough so that the shops didn't merge together, and she wanted each one to be a part of the picture while remaining separate. The barber pole was taking shape with its bright red and white swirls. In front of the grocery, there was a fruit and vegetable display. She put Fitz out front arranging his apples. Next door, Mrs. Burdock, with her big apron, was washing her front window. Doc Stanton's had a sign with the caduceus over his doorway. Through the barbershop window, Pete Bradshaw could be seen giving a haircut. Then there was Mr. Mobley sweeping the sidewalk in front of his hardware store. Last but not least, there was Captured Moments. Jodi even painted an easel in the front window with a painting on it. The faces on the shopkeepers were very warm to the viewer. It was clear just by looking at this town that it was a welcoming place.

"That's exactly what I want the viewer to feel," said Jodi to herself.

A few finishing touches, and it would be done. Dave came in to take a look at it.

"Wow, sweetie! You've done it again. I love it!" he said.

"I like it too, hon. It's very different from my others," she said.

"You're very versatile. You should try all kinds of subjects."

"I do enjoy a challenge," she said.

Chapter 55

The Sea Bird had some new guests for the week. Heywood and Alice Livingston were from Washington D.C. He had just retired from his position as state senator, and Alice said they were looking for a place where he could relax. Susan assured her that he would have no problems doing that at the Sea Bird.

"That front porch is calling me to come right on up and sit down," chuckled Heywood.

When Alex heard that, he said, "Let's get your bags into your room, and you can do just that. Sit as long as your heart desires!"

"Heywood's doctor recommended a *very* relaxing rest," said Alice.

"We'll see to that," said Alex. "He can do as little as he wants. I'll have Sarah, our cook, bring out some drinks and a snack while you enjoy the view."

"That sounds wonderful," said Alice.

The next day, Fred Carpenter came in from Dallas. He was a rancher who had come to Georgia on business. He had decided to take a side trip for a day or two just to get away from it all. Fred got there in the afternoon. When he saw the Livingstons on the front porch, he said, "Now don't that look homey! Mind if I join you?"

"No, not all," they replied.

"Let me get settled in, and I will be right out," he told them.

Susan checked him in, and Dave carried his bags to his room.

"Would you like a drink and a snack on the porch?" Susan asked.

"I'd just love that," he told her.

"I'll have Sarah bring it right out to you."

"Thank you, ma'am."

Fred found himself a rocker and sat down on the porch, and Sarah came out with his food.

"Now I could get used to this," he chuckled. "Thank you kindly."

"You are most welcome," replied Sarah.

Fred and the Livingstons sat discussing the inn and what a lovely view it had of the ocean.

"I came here to get a break from my business, and I think I have found just the right spot," Fred told them.

"The Bennetts are wonderful innkeepers," said Alice.

"The food is delicious, too, although it probably won't help my waistline," chuckled Heywood.

"I never watch my waistline," said Fred with a laugh. "It does whatever it wants to."

They sat watching as the sun began to sink out over the ocean.

"Just beautiful. Absolutely beautiful," Alice said.

"It surely is ma'am," agreed Fred.

At supper that night, everyone was enjoying Sarah's cooking. She served sweet potatoes, roast beef, steamed onions, and green beans. For dessert, they had cherry cobbler with whipped cream.

"My compliments to the chef," said Fred. "My cook back home doesn't come close to this, ma'am."

Sarah poked her head out of the kitchen. "We aim to please!"

"Well, I can tell you, little missy, *your* aim is just dandy!" he laughed.

Chapter 56

The finishing touches were all done now on *Welcome to Windy Point,* and Dave had convinced Jodi to put the painting in the window to show it off. The first thing that morning, that was what she did. It did look rather nice to see it there. It showed well from outside, too.

By noon, Dave noticed that a steady flow of people had gathered in front of the shop. Some came alone and then reappeared with someone else. After a while, Jodi realized what was happening. They were coming to see the Windy Point painting.

In the group, she saw Mr. Mobley, Mrs. Bradock, Doc Stanton, Mr. Bradshaw, and Fitz—all subjects in the painting.

Dave and Jodi stepped outside.

"Well, what do you think?" asked Jodi.

"*We love it!*" they all said together.

"I want to buy it, Jodi," said Mr. Mobley.

"No, I want it!" said Mrs. Burdock.

"Well we can't *all* have it," said Fitz.

Ben Dawson stepped out of the crowd. "I have a suggestion. What if the town of Windy Point were to buy it and display it for everyone?" he said.

"That's a terrific idea!" said Mrs. Burdock.

"That way we can all enjoy it," Ben said. "I'm on the Chamber of Commerce, and I think we can get it with some of the funds used for promoting our town's tourism. This painting will make people want to visit Windy Point."

The group was now applauding this idea.

"Save that painting, Jodi," said Ben. "I'll get back to you."

"That's wonderful, Mr. Dawson. I sure will," said Jodi.

After the crowd had gone, she went back inside. She couldn't stop smiling.

"Jodi, you make me so proud," Dave told her.

"If I wasn't a happy wife, I wouldn't be a happy artist," she said with a grin.

◊◊◊

Alex and Susan were thrilled to hear about the townspeople loving Jodi's painting.

"I haven't even seen it yet," said Susan.

"You'll have to drive into town to see it," said Dave. "We have it in the window. That's what got the excitement started."

"That's so cool!" said Jesse. "A riot over my sister's painting."

"Well, let's not call it a 'riot,'" said Jodi. "It was exciting, though."

As they climbed into bed that night they talked again about her painting.

"You have such a knack, Jodi," said Dave. "It seems like you do well with everything you try."

"Well, I wonder if I will be a great mom," she said.

"Why do you say that, sweetie? Of course you will."

"I just wonder because I think I just had a labor pain."

"*What*? Are you sure?"

"I don't know, but I've never felt anything like that before. Maybe it was all the excitement today, or it could have been just the baby kicking again. Let's just see if anything else happens."

It wasn't easy, but they tried to relax and get some sleep. An hour passed, and Jodi got up to go to the bathroom. When she stood up, another pain hit her in the belly.

"Ow, ow, ow!" she said.

"Sweetie! Are you okay?"

"I think my water just broke," she told him.

"Let me get your Mom," he told her.

"Yeah, she will know if we need to call Doc Stanton yet," she said.

She lay back down on the bed while Dave went to get Susan. Dave tapped lightly on their bedroom door.

"Susan! Susan! I think Jodi may be in labor!" he said.

Susan came quickly to the door. "I'll be right there, Dave," she said.

When the two of them got back to Jodi, she was having another pain.

"How close, Jodi?" asked Susan.

"About fifteen minutes, I think."

"When did they start?"

"About an hour and a half ago," said Dave.

"Let's see how close the next one is before we call the doctor," she told them.

By now, Alex had come into the room. "Are you okay, sweetheart?" he asked.

"Yes, dad," said Jodi. "It's just starting."

Jodi had just gotten comfortable on the bed when another one hit. This one was a little stronger.

"That's less than fifteen minutes," said Mom. "I think it might be a good idea to call Doc Stanton. It will take him a while to get here."

"His phone number is beside the phone."

The group stayed in the room, watching to see what would happen next. Dave paced the floor, trying to stay calm. Sarah and Jesse were downstairs waiting for the doctor. Sparky started barking when he saw the doctor's headlights coming in the driveway. A moment later, Doc Stanton came in and said, "Where is our little mama?"

"Follow me, Doc," said Dave.

"Jodi, how are we doing?" he said as he entered the room.

"I'm not really sure, Doc," said Jodi. "I feel like I have to go use the bathroom."

"That sounds like we won't have long to wait," he told her.

◊◊◊

For the next two hours, Jodi felt the baby coming. She tried hard not to cry out, but it wasn't easy. Dave sat with her, stroking her hair.

"Hold on, sweetie, I'm here," he said.

"Okay, Jodi," said Doc Stanton. "One more good push should do it. Give it a good one, honey."

"*Oh!*" she yelled, and as she did, out came a beautiful baby boy.

"It's a boy! It's a boy!" yelled Dave. "Oh, sweetie, I love you so much!"

Susan cried as she clung to Alex, who was trying to hide his tears. Sarah stood dabbing her eyes with a tissue. Jesse looked so proud to be an uncle. Sparky clearly knew something exciting had just happened, but he wasn't sure what.

"Jodi, you did great, and you delivered a fine little boy," said Doc Stanton. "Seven pounds, six ounces." Then he said goodbye, saying he would return to check her again in the morning.

Dave and Jodi decided to name the baby after both of their fathers. It was to be David Alexander Langley, and he would be called Davie. They were certainly two proud parents.

Jodi stood, admiring the little boy in the crib his father had built for him. She picked him up and held him close to her.

"I have waited for you for so long, little one," she said. "I cannot *wait* to put you on canvas! *You* are my Captured Moment."

CPSIA information can be obtained
at www.ICGtesting.com
Printed in the USA
LVOW04s0307091116
512190LV00010BA/126/P